D1446623

THE FINAL BID

The Auction Series, Book Two

MICHELLE WINDSOR

First published April 2017
Copyright ©Michelle Windsor 2017
Published by
Windsor House Publishing
Cover design by Jessica Hildreth at Creative Book Concepts
Cover bouquet designed by Amanda Walker Design Services
A special thank you to Nasar Jewelers in Plaistow, NH, for allowing me to borrow and photograph the wedding ring set displayed on the cover.
Developmental and copy editing provided by the amazing Elizabeth Nover at Razor Sharp Editing

This is for everyone who ever wanted to write a story and didn't think they could.
I'm living proof that you can.
Go chase those dreams—every single one of them!

PROLOGUE

Drew leaned against the brick wall of the alley, his breath leaving him in puffy white clouds. Fall temperatures had finally arrived and mornings were dawning chillier each day. He pulled the hood of his sweatshirt tighter over his head and then stuffed his hands into the front pocket to save some of the warmth his body had created during his run. This morning, he'd arrived earlier than usual and had been waiting in the alley across from the flower shop for almost half an hour.

It had been four days since he'd run into her in the lobby of his hotel. Four days since he'd discovered she had a child and a husband. *Is it her husband? Is she even married?* She had specifically said she wouldn't have been at Baton Timide if she were married. The last four days had been full of gut-twisting agony as he'd wondered.

He shouldn't be here, it was wrong. Still, each morning, here he was, hidden in the shadows like a thief, waiting to steal another glance of her. Scarlett. *Hannah.* There were so many questions he wanted to ask her, but four days ago, when she'd looked straight at him and said "No," she had made it crystal clear she didn't want to see him again.

Yet he was here anyway, waiting and watching. Trying to figure out what to do next but needing to see her in the meantime. As the door in the alley opened, he pushed himself further into the shadows, his heart beating violently in his chest. Hannah stepped out, and then a second, smaller version of her shuffled out, waiting while her mother locked the door. His eyes remained fixed on Hannah as she took her daughter's hand to guide her out of the alley before buckling her into their van and driving away.

Twenty minutes later, like the previous mornings, the now familiar van pulled back into the alley beside the shop. The brake lights flashed red as the sound of the engine died. The van door opened and closed, and then Hannah emerged between the wall and the van.

Today she wore a black wool coat, a bright pink scarf wrapped around her neck, her nose buried in its warmth as she hurried to the front door of the flower shop. Her loose and wavy hair, the color of gold, flowed down over her back, contrasting starkly with the coat. If he could get close enough, he knew she would smell like flowers.

Drew continued to watch as she unlocked the metal casing covering the door, then slid it up and out of the way. The metal must have been cold because she rubbed her hands together and blew on them. She found another key in the set she held and unlocked the interior door of the shop. The faint tinkling of the bell carried on the breeze as she shut the door behind her.

He stayed another thirty minutes, waiting to see if this morning would be any different than the last three. It wasn't. Her coworker arrived just before eight a.m., followed by a delivery truck full of flowers a few minutes later. He popped his earbuds back in, pushed play on his iPod, put his head down and began the run back to the hotel before she came out to meet the delivery driver.

CHAPTER ONE

"Grace Victoria Rose, you better have your coat on!" Hannah walked through the kitchen of her apartment and out into the hallway. Sure enough, her daughter was hiding behind the jackets hanging in a line by the front door, instead of putting herself into one.

"Gracie, what in the world are you doing?" Hannah knelt down and gently pulled her daughter out from behind the coats.

"Honey, we're going to be late. Why are you hiding?" Hannah grabbed a small lavender coat off one of the hooks.

"Momma, I don't want to go to school today," Her little voice pouty and sad

"Sweetie, did you forget what today is?" Hannah swiftly pulled her daughter's coat on, buttoned it up and then stood. "Did you forget someone's birthday?"

Her face scrunched up in thought, and then, just as quickly, a large smile broke across her face. "I remember now! It's Daddy's birthday!"

Hannah bent down again to wrap a dark purple scarf around her daughter's young neck. November had come in like a lion and each morning was colder than the last.

"That's right!" She finished wrapping the scarf and then kissed the tip of Grace's nose. "So, I'll pick you up at eleven, and then you can come help me with the flowers before we go see him, okay?"

The little girl jumped up and down in excitement. "Okay, Momma."

"Okay. We gotta go now, Peanut. Grab your backpack." Hannah pointed to a small pink backpack sitting on a bench next to the front door, then grabbed her purse and keys off one of the wall hooks. She ushered Grace out the door, through the alley and into the delivery van. After dropping Grace off at the daycare center she attended daily, she drove the short distance back to the flower shop.

As she unlocked the door to The Secret Garden, she was still in a state of disbelief that it would be hers in just a few short days. A month ago, she had told Donna, the current owner, she couldn't come up with the down payment and would have to pass on purchasing the shop. Then, just three days ago, Donna had called and dropped a bombshell: she'd changed her mind and would like to sell the shop to Hannah in a private sale. She wanted to provide Hannah this opportunity and couldn't see anyone else taking over "her baby." They would work out a monthly payment plan that was beneficial to both of them.

The shop specialized in elegant extravagance and had an extensive clientele that included many of the wealthiest residents in New York. Hannah was thrilled to be able to keep working with her existing clients, but even more excited to finally have something to call her own; something that would allow her to raise her daughter comfortably.

The very best part of the purchase was that she was getting the entire building. That meant the apartment above the shop was now going to be hers as well. She breathed a sigh of relief that things were finally taking a turn for the better. At that precise thought, her eyes fell on the black silk mask sitting discreetly on the shelf above her desk. On second thought, maybe not everything had worked out as she'd expected.

She still couldn't believe that she had run into Drew Sapphire while making a delivery earlier that week, and, that he was the heir to the Sapphire Luxury Resort chain. She felt incredibly stupid for not putting two and two together before then, but after the way they'd parted, her only desire had been to try and push him to the back of her mind.

She sighed heavily as she removed her scarf and coat, hanging them up in the small closet in the back room. She walked to her desk, picking up the business card that Drew had enclosed in the note he'd sent two months ago, and sat down. She ran her fingers over the slightly raised sapphire font that spelled out his name before bringing the card to her nose. Closing her eyes and inhaling, she swore she could still catch the faintest trace of his scent after all this time. It was a crisp, clean, woodsy aroma that she couldn't seem to escape. No matter how hard she tried to put her feelings for Drew in a tightly locked box, every night when she closed her eyes, he was all that she could see.

He invaded her dreams, every nerve coming alive with the memory of the way he'd touched her, kissed her, licked her. She would wake up drenched in sweat, aching for his touch, her body pulsing for him. And every day since she'd seen him, she kept waiting for him to walk through the shop door and confront her. But each day went by without any trace of him. She couldn't erase the memory of his shocked face when she'd scooped her daughter up into her arms. Her child had finally given him a reason to stop pursuing her. Which is what she'd wanted, after all. At least, that's what she kept telling herself.

"Hannah? Hello? Anyone home in there?" Robin stood in front of her. Hannah hadn't even heard the bells on the door when her assistant had arrived.

Hannah stood up and gave her friend a quick hug good morning. "Robin, hey! Sorry, I was so deep in thought about that arrangement we need to do for the Penn's order that I didn't even hear you come in."

"No worries, sweetie. I brought you a tea from Oslo's."

Robin handed her a white to-go cup, then placed her things on the counter so she could remove her jacket and hang it up.

Hannah took the tea and smiled in gratitude. "Thanks, you're too good to me. Let's go see if Tony's here with the deliveries yet."

F our hours later, with morning orders complete and Grace back at the shop, Hannah glanced at her watch. She needed to leave soon to take Grace to see Jackson. They had to drive out to Brooklyn, and the afternoon traffic would be a challenge. She walked out of the work room into the front of the shop and found Grace sitting on a stool and working on a bouquet at the counter with Sara, one of the other women that worked for her.

Grace's voice pulled her from her thoughts. "Look what I made for Daddy, Momma!"

Grace proudly held up a large bouquet of white chrysanthemums wrapped in a red felt ribbon. "Sara said we should use these because they are the flower for November and they are perfect for Daddy."

Hannah took the bouquet from her daughter's small hands, held it up to her nose and inhaled deeply. "It's beautiful, Gracie. Daddy will love them."

Hannah looked up and smiled in thanks at Sara. "You okay if I head out now? All the orders have been prepped for the rest of the afternoon deliveries and pickups, and Josh will be back to get those around one thirty."

"Of course," Sara replied while helping Grace down off her stool. "I'll take care of everything and lock up at five. Just call me if you think of anything else."

"I will, thanks." She reached a hand out to Grace. "You ready, Peanut?"

Grace grabbed her mother's hand and followed her into the back room. They both bundled up in their coats and then proceeded back through the shop and out the front door to their van.

The Grand Central Parkway would probably be the best route into Brooklyn this time of day. It was less than twenty miles to their destination, but with traffic, it could easily take them an hour. Not that the time ever passed slowly when she was in the car with Grace. She was a chatter bug with one tale after another about her morning at Miss Daisy's and how excited she was to go to her Auntie Tammy's on Sunday to play with her cousin Emma. Before Hannah knew it, she was pulling through the gates and putting the van into park. She got out and unbuckled Grace, lifting her out of her seat to place her on the sidewalk before handing her the bouquet.

"Want to go find Daddy? Do you remember where he is?"

"I think so, Momma. Follow me!" Grace turned and ran, Hannah close on her heels.

Grace stopped, turned in a circle, looked to her right and then took off again. "I found him, Momma!"

Hannah walked up behind her daughter, placing both hands on her shoulders, squeezing gently. "Yes you did. You're so smart."

Hannah smiled sadly as her young, sweet, innocent daughter bent down to place the bouquet on the ground next to her father's grave before kissing the white stone. "Happy birthday, Daddy."

As Gracie stood back up, she pointed to the top of the head-stone. "Look, Momma, someone else brought Daddy a flower too."

The single black rose contrasted with the simple ivory of the military headstone. She wondered about who had left it. It wasn't the first time she'd found one on his grave. Her eyes lowered away from the flower as she scanned the simple script on the stone.

JACKSON T ROSE
SGT, US ARMY
NOV 7 1985 - JUN 10 2013
PURPLE HEART

BRONZE STAR
OPERATION IRAQI FREEDOM

It was hard for her to believe that he'd been gone for almost two and a half years now. He would have been thirty years old today. She bent down and ran her fingers over the engraved letters of his name. "Happy birthday, baby. I miss you every day."

She took a key out of her pocket and placed it in the dirt against the gravestone. "I did it, Jackson. We said by the time you turned thirty, and I did it."

It was silly to leave the key, but it was her way of letting him know that she had followed through on their dream of owning a home and business. She stood, brushing the loose dirt off the knees of her jeans, turning her attention back to her daughter. Grace was weaving through the gravestones, touching each one as she went saying, "Thank you." Her heart swelled with love and gratitude for the gift of her daughter and the kindness her young soul already possessed.

She called out, "Gracie! You ready to go get some pizza and cake?"

Grace's head swung in her mother's direction, her face lighting up with a smile as she turned and skipped closer. "Can we get ice cream too, Momma?"

Hannah smiled. "Uh, yeah! We can't have cake without ice cream!"

"Yay!" Grace jumped up and down with excitement before zipping her way back to the van, both of them climbing in for the trip back home.

CHAPTER TWO

It was day five, and Drew was done with just watching. When Hannah started unlocking the metal casing, he left the cover of the alley and crossed the street. His sneakers were silent on the pavement, making it easy for him to come up behind her with no warning. She slid the metal casing up, unlocked the front door and pulled it open.

He was two steps behind her as he slid through, bells tinkling overhead. Humming distractedly, she still hadn't realized that he was there. Her humming stopped him cold. "Into the Mystic." The song they had danced to at his beach house.

"Hannah." His voice was low and gruff. His palms were sweating and his pulse was in overdrive. She shrieked in surprise as she spun around, her eyes growing wide when they landed on him.

"Holy shit, Drew! What the hell are you doing here?" Her hand flew up to her chest, as if to still her heart, before her face darkened in anger. "Are you trying to give me a goddamn heart attack?"

He took a step closer, then stopped when she took two steps back. He pushed the hood of his sweatshirt off as he raked his fingers through his hair, lowering his hands to his waist, palms up, to show her he meant no harm. "I'm sorry. I just—" He shook his head, blinking once before continuing. "Jesus, Hannah. I'd forgotten how beautiful you are."

She stared at him, her features softening as she let out a sigh. "Drew, what are you doing here?"

"I want—" He paused, frowning. "I need to talk to you."

She unwrapped the scarf from her neck and then unbuttoned her coat. She said nothing as she hung them up in the closet. "I'm not really sure there's anything to say."

His eyes followed her as she settled on the opposite side of the work table from him.

"What do you mean there's nothing to say? I saw you with your daughter and husband. Is he your ex-husband? You said you weren't married, but are you? I haven't seen him here since that day." He raked a hand through his disheveled hair again, his eyes darting around her wildly.

Hannah's eyes narrowed. "What do you mean, you haven't seen him here? Have you been watching me?"

He took a deep breath. *Damn it, he'd gone this far, might as well keep going.* "I'm just trying to understand who you are and what the hell happened between us. Because I know for certain, it wasn't like anything I've ever experienced before."

He took a couple steps around the table to get closer to her, but she countered his action, keeping a large space between them. "Do you think about me at all?"

Her expression remained blank. He drummed his fingers heavily on the table in frustration. "Because I can't stop thinking of you. It's been over two months, and I can't get you out of my system. And believe me, I've tried."

She raised one eyebrow, distaste evident in her tone as she replied. "Girls at Baton Timide helping out with that?"

He scoffed, rolling his eyes. "Try tequila. Lots and lots of it."

He locked his gaze angrily on hers and rounded the table. "You think another woman is the answer to my problem? You think if I go to the club and buy myself someone new, tie them up, and fuck them, that I'll forget the way you felt?" He prowled closer. "That I'll forget how you smell, how you taste?"

Drew had reached her now and grasped her by the shoulders as he whispered in her ear. "That I'll forget how you screamed my name as I drove myself into you?"

Her breathing quickened as he ran his nose from her ear into the soft tresses of her hair, inhaling her scent. He was about to pull away when she turned her head, her lips brushing across his. Before he could stop himself, he put a hand on her cheek and crushed his mouth against hers, sliding his tongue across its seam, forcing her to open up to him. She hesitated for only a second before her mouth parted on a moan, her tongue meeting his, her hands bunching the material of his sweatshirt.

He dropped his hand from her face to grab her waist, pulling her body close, their kiss growing deeper, more desperate. He lifted her onto the table, her legs wrapping around him, her hips thrusting forward as her core ground against his. With one hand tangled in her hair and their mouths fused together in desire, he used his other hand to palm her ass, thrusting his cock harder against her pussy.

He hadn't been with anyone since Hannah, and if they kept this up, he was going to explode in a matter of minutes. To slow things down, he tore his lips away from hers and began peppering kisses along her neck. She whimpered in protest but then groaned softly, her head falling back on her shoulders, her long hair brushing against the table. He cupped her breast and rolled her taut nipple between his fingers, reveling in the sounds coming from her throat. Sounds he hadn't known he would ever hear again.

She arched her back into his touch, pushing her center more forcefully against his throbbing cock. "Fuck, Hannah," he hissed, leaning down, fusing his lips to hers again. He reached under her shirt and yanked down the cup covering her breast. He ran his thumb back and forth over the peak of her nipple, elongating with each stroke.

She broke their kiss with a moan. "Drew . . ."

He moved his mouth against her ear. "I've waited two months to hear you say my name like that again." And then trailed his lips back across to hers, sealing them together once more.

"Oh holy shit! Sorry!" A girl's voice rang out in surprise behind Drew. Hannah's coworker had come in and neither had heard her or the bell on the door.

Drew quickly pulled himself off Hannah as she simultaneously pushed him away as she moved off the table. He turned in an attempt to hide his still-erect member as she fumbled her clothes back into their proper position behind him.

A very red-faced girl in her young twenties, whom Drew recognized from his morning stakeouts, was standing in the entryway to the back room, her hand held tightly over her eyes. "I'm just going to go out to the coffee shop."

She started backing out of the doorway, her other hand feeling her way behind her. "I'll be back later. Didn't see a thing! I swear!" And then turned and fled out the front door.

Drew took a step toward Hannah, frustrated at his loss of control. "I'm sorry. I didn't mean to put you in that position."

She shook her head as if trying to clear it, shoving her hand out flat in front of her. "No, I'm sorry. I shouldn't have let that happen."

Disappointment bled into his voice. "But it did. And you can't deny that you don't feel something for me. I deserve some answers, Hannah."

"I know you do." She sighed in defeat. "But, Drew, not now. Please, just go. I'm begging you."

He took two steps forward, butting up against her hand, and then stopped. "This isn't over."

'I know' fell from her lips in a whisper before he stormed past her and through the shop, slamming the door behind him.

THE FINAL BID • 13

F our hours later, and probably four miles of pacing back and forth in his office, and he wasn't any less frustrated than when he'd left Hannah that morning. *What the fuck was I thinking, confronting her like that? But Jesus, did it feel good to have her in my arms again.*

A buzzing from the intercom interrupted his thoughts, stopping him in his tracks. He changed direction and pushed the button to respond. "I thought I said no calls, Felicia."

"Sir, it's Hannah. I thought you'd want to take this."

God damn, my assistant is good. "Yes, put her through, please. Thank you."

His heart rate picked up as he sat down in front of his desk. He blew out a long breath and then picked up the receiver.

"Hannah?" His voice was deep and low, hopefully hiding his nerves.

"Yes, hello, Drew." She did sound nervous, which in a strange way comforted him.

"I wasn't sure if it was really going to be you on the other line."

"Surprised?" She laughed lightly.

"Relieved." There was a moment of silence before Drew continued. "I've been pacing around my office since I left you this morning. I shouldn't have ambushed you like that. I'm sorry. I really just wanted some answers. To understand."

She murmured, "I know. I'm sorry too. This is as confusing to me as it is to you."

"Can we meet? I'd like to talk."

"That's why I'm calling. I'd like to meet with you too. To try and explain."

"Okay, I can be there in twenty minutes," he responded, rising out of his chair.

"No, I can't today. I'm working and I have my daughter every evening."

Frustration cut him to the core, his free hand dragging roughly through his hair as he tried to rein in his disappointment.

"Okay. When? I'll make myself available any time that works for you."

"I can meet you on Sunday. The shop is closed that day. Will that work?"

"What time?" Sunday felt like fucking forever, but if that's what she had to give, he would take it.

"Is eleven okay?"

"Any time is fine. I can do eleven. Should I meet you at the shop? Pick you up?"

"No, not here. Someplace else."

"Okay. I'll have a car pick you up at ten forty-five and bring you to my place."

A large sigh came through the receiver. "Drew, I can't go out to the Hamptons. It's too far and I don't have that much time."

"No, not my house. I keep a suite at the hotel when I'm in town working."

"Oh, okay, but I don't need a car. I'll get myself there."

"Hannah, just let me send a car." His controlling nature was clearly trying to take charge.

"No. Don't send one or I won't come."

He growled into the phone. Actually growled. "You are so infuriating sometimes. Fine. No car."

"Thank you." There was a pause as she took a breath before continuing. "Which one?"

"Which one what?" Confusion evident in his tone.

"Which hotel is your suite at? There are four Sapphire Resorts in Manhattan."

He would bet his life that she was rolling her eyes. "Ah, yes. Sorry. The one on West Fifty-Ninth. Just let the front desk know when you arrive."

"Okay. I'll see you then."

"Hannah?"

"Yes?"

He wanted to keep her on the phone longer, but didn't want to push her away now that she was almost in his grasp, so he kept it simple. "Thank you for meeting with me."

"Yep." A click sounded, and Drew looked in disbelief at the receiver in his hand as the dull sound of the dial tone came across the line.

She'd hung up on him before he could say goodbye. *Goddamn stubborn woman is going to be the end of me.* He slammed the receiver back into the cradle and then rolled the chair back from his desk, swiveling toward the window as he grumbled under his breath.

His office was on the thirteenth floor of the hotel, overlooking Central Park. It was mid-afternoon and chilly out, so there wasn't a lot of foot traffic or people waiting for the horse-drawn carriages that lined the street. A woman emerged from the park, a young girl holding her hand and skipping beside her; both of them had blonde hair. They could have easily been Hannah and her daughter. How many times had they passed right under his window without his ever knowing?

A week ago, he definitely wouldn't have noticed the duo. Had he been better off in that blissful state of ignorance than with the knowledge he had now? Instead of pondering the question further, he twirled his chair back around to his desk and brought up a chat session on his computer. He pulled up his brother Benny's profile and started typing.

Hey, you there?

Several moments passed without a response, and Drew was about to grab his cell phone to call instead, when a return message popped up.

What's up?

He quickly typed a response.

Wanna go blow off some steam?

It was only a few seconds before another reply came.

Sure, I'll pick you up in ten.

It was only Friday afternoon and Sunday seemed a long way off. Patience wasn't his strong suit, and if he didn't get out of his own head, he might go mad. Benny always knew how to bring him back down to level ground again. He shut down his laptop, put his phone in his pocket and grabbed his jacket out of the closet before exiting his office. Felicia looked up from her desk as he shut his door.

"Leaving for the day?" She was a pretty woman, with long, straight auburn hair and big green eyes. She had started working for him about six months ago and had turned out to be one of the best assistants he'd had to date.

"Yes. Do I have anything important on the schedule?"

She quickly brought up his calendar on the computer and, after a glance, looked up at him with a frown. "Your father. Status meeting for the Boston hotel at four."

"Okay, I'll handle that. If he happens to call to confirm, just tell him I can't make it and I'll be in touch." He typed a quick reminder into his phone about calling his dad. "Anything else?"

Felicia shook her head. "No, sir. Nothing that I can't work or move around for you."

"Excellent. You're the best." He smiled and started walking toward the exit. "I'll be with Ben, and I'll have my cell if you need me for any emergencies."

"Very good, sir." Felicia smiled and nodded her head in farewell. "Have a good weekend."

"Thanks, you too."

Drew made his way down the hall to the elevator, taking it to the ground floor to wait for Benny. As he crossed the lobby, he pulled his jacket on over his dark suit, wishing he had thought to change into something more casual. He checked his watch. Did he have time to run up to his suite? But there was Benny pulling up in front of the hotel. He shook his head at his brother's typical choice in car, a Dodge Challenger SRT Hellcat in black. A straight-up muscle car.

The doorman tipped his hat as Drew walked through the exit and across the sidewalk to Benny's car. He pulled open the passenger door and slid into the caramel-colored leather seat.

Benny gunned the engine with a grin and sped into traffic as soon as Drew's door was shut.

"Hey, Brother."

"Hey yourself. Thanks for grabbing me."

Ben shrugged. "Sure. What's up? Dad?"

Drew shook his head and blew out a long breath. "Nope. Dad's easy compared to this."

Ben raised an eyebrow. "This have anything to do with Scarlett?"

"Hannah," Drew corrected.

"Who's Hannah?" Ben asked, confused.

"Scarlett," Drew replied.

"What?" Ben's brow now furrowed.

"Scarlett is really Hannah." Drew stated like it should be obvious.

"What the fuck? You're making no sense."

"Tell me about it." Drew shook his head. "I don't want to talk about it."

"Alrighty then." Ben reached over and turned the radio up to drown out some of the silence in the car.

"You said you had something in mind?" Drew shouted over the music.

Ben glanced at his brother as he weaved through traffic and over the bridge into Brooklyn, a big grin spreading across his face. "How do you feel about a little boxing?"

Drew grinned back, a surge of excitement running through him. "Hell, yeah."

"Perfect. I know some guys who will be happy to help you work out some of your shit."

"Why do I get the sense you're looking forward to seeing me get my ass beat?"

Ben reached over, ruffling Drew's perfectly coifed hair. "Cause that's what big brothers are for."

Drew leaned away, punching his brother lightly in the arm. "Yeah, whatever."

"Seriously, these are all good guys. I just gotta make a quick stop at Cypress Hills while we're in Brooklyn. You mind?"

"Nope." Drew looked over at his brother. "Whatever you need."

He had forty-six more fucking hours to kill before seeing Hannah.

CHAPTER THREE

Hannah entered the lobby of the hotel and walked toward the concierge desk. Her heart was beating hard enough to drown out the clacking of her boot heels on the marble. She had changed no less than four times before finally deciding on a pair of boyfriend-style jeans (with perfectly ripped patches, of course), a simple black off-the-shoulder T-shirt, an old leather jacket and black ankle booties. Just an outfit she would normally wear to visit with friends. For this meeting, she wanted to be in her own skin, not in what Drew would want to see.

She smiled as she reached the concierge desk. George, her favorite clerk at this hotel, was on duty this morning. "Good morning, George."

"Hannah! Good morning to you! Are you working on a Sunday?"

She shook her head, her cheeks flushing as she responded, "No. I actually have an appointment with Drew—er, Mr. Sapphire at eleven. I'm a bit early though."

She glanced down at her watch. She was a whole fifteen minutes early. Argh, now I look too anxious.

George smiled warmly and picked up the phone. "Let me call

up to see if he's available now. He just came back from a run not too long ago."

She glanced around, taking in the sights and sounds of people making their way through the lobby, wondering where people might be visiting from or where they were heading to. George came around the desk and touched her lightly on the elbow, guiding her toward a set of elevators.

"If you'll come with me? Mr. Sapphire's on a secure floor, so I'll just need to punch in an access code."

"Of course." She followed George and stood silently as they both waited for the elevator to arrive. He swept his hand out, inviting her to enter the elevator first. He held the door open as he quickly entered a code on a keypad, then pressed PH3 and stepped back out.

"Off you go then, miss." He tipped his head and smiled as the doors slid shut.

Hannah raised a hand in goodbye and got out a quick thank you before the doors shut and the elevator started to rise. Her heart, which had calmed a bit while speaking with George, increased its rate with every floor she climbed. This was a moment she had hoped never to find herself in, but it would be unfair to herself, and Drew, not to give him some kind of closure to their weekend. She scoffed a bit at that. He was the one that had stormed out on her and left her alone and confused in his house.

The elevator came to a quick stop, a ding indicating her arrival, and the doors slid open. She took a deep breath before stepping out into the foyer of the suite—and right into Drew's steely blue gaze. She stopped abruptly, a small gasp escaping her lips. *Why does he have to look so damn delicious?*

He was leaning against the wall, just feet away from the elevator's entrance, wearing faded jeans and a light gray, fitted T-shirt. His toned arms were crossed, as were his bare feet, his hair still wet from a recent shower.

"What happened to your eye?" she asked in concern. She took

a few steps closer and reached up, but then stopped short before touching his face.

"Hello, Hannah." He pushed himself off the wall, watching as her hand slowly sank back down to her side, then kissed her softly on the cheek. "You're early." He let out a small scoff. "Anxious as ever?"

His stubble-lined jaw held that sly grin she had quickly come to know over the weekend they'd spent together. She frowned slightly at his brush-off. "Drew, your eye? What happened? Are you okay?"

"I'm fine. It's nothing. A little reminder that I'm not as good at boxing as I used to be." He turned and started walking down a short hallway, motioning for her to follow. "Come, let's go sit in the dining room. I ordered some food in case you're hungry."

She followed him down a hallway that opened into a large space containing a kitchen, a dining room and a seating area. Three walls were nothing but windows, allowing the bright sunshine of the day to light up the room. He walked over to a table filled with several silver-covered platters and pulled out a chair for her.

"Can I take your jacket?"

"Sure, thanks." She shrugged out of her jacket and handed it to him before sitting down in the seat. He laid it over the arm of a nearby couch and walked back to the table. As he passed her, his fingers skimmed ever so softly over her bare shoulder, and then he sat down in the seat next to her. He stared at her, quiet for several moments.

"What is it?" Hannah looked down at herself, checking to see if something was on her shirt.

He chuckled, his cheeks dimpling as they lifted. "I always forget how beautiful you are. Every time I see you, I'm reminded."

Hannah's cheeks heated in embarrassment. "Does your eye hurt?" This time, she did reach up and brush her fingertips over the bruise.

He took her hand in his own, his expression turning serious.

"I'm sure it's nothing compared to the pain I must have caused when I left you at the beach house."

Her eyebrows shot up in surprise. She'd been sure he would evade that subject in pursuit of her secrets. She tilted her head in thought before answering. "Confused, and yes, I suppose hurt. I didn't really want to believe that you would just leave after, well . . . after everything we shared together."

Drew scooted his chair closer, his knee bumping into hers, while still holding her hand. "I'm so sorry about that. For losing my temper. For not respecting your privacy. For leaving you. You were trying to meet me in the middle and I had to go and take more from you. I know it wasn't fair."

She looked past Drew and stared blankly out the window behind him as she tried to register his apology. It wasn't what she'd expected from him, and it was throwing her off-balance. *Why did he have to be so goddamn nice?*

"Hannah?" Drew's voice pulled her out of her thoughts. "Are you okay?"

She stood quickly, sliding her hand from Drew's. He stood up just as quickly in response. "Can I use the bathroom please?"

A look of confusion crossed his features. "Um, of course." He pointed toward a hallway off the kitchen. "It's the first door on the right."

"Thanks. Just be a minute."

D rew watched as Hannah escaped down the hallway into the bathroom, shutting the door firmly behind her. He ran a hand through his hair before shaking his head in confusion. *What the fuck was that about?* Unsure what to do but feeling the need to keep busy, he poured each of them a mimosa, then started removing the covers from all the platters.

He stacked them on the counter and then went back and sat at the table to wait. A moment later, the door of the bathroom clicked open and Hannah's footsteps padded toward him. Would she leave now?

"Are you—"

"I'm sorry—"

They both laughed nervously. He stood. "Are you okay?"

"Yes, yes." She looked down as embarrassment flooded her cheeks. "I needed a minute. I just . . ."

He waited for her to continue, but when she didn't, he placed a finger under her chin, raising it so he could look her in the eyes. "You just what?"

"I just wasn't expecting that." Her voice timid as her cheeks heated.

"That?" Drew scratched the stubble on his chin. "What do you mean?"

She took a step back, breaking their connection. "I wasn't expecting you to apologize. To take any responsibility for your actions that evening. To acknowledge that you hadn't respected my need for some control over my situation."

Astonished, he couldn't help chuckling. "Has no man ever apologized to you before? Your husband?"

She shook her head, a wry smile appearing. "I was wondering when you were going to bring that up."

"Well, you must know seeing you with a man and a child would shock me. Your husband and daughter, I presume?"

He sat back down at the table, motioning for her to do the same. He lifted the flute of one mimosa to his mouth, draining it in a single gulp.

Hannah's expression saddened as she took a small sip from the drink sitting in front of her. "Yes, that was my daughter you saw me with. Grace. She's four, almost five now. But that wasn't my husband. It was my brother."

Relief surged through his bloodstream and straight to his heart, flooding it with hope. He forced himself not to break into a grin as he continued questioning her. "Your brother? He's in the military? I noticed he was wearing fatigues."

"He's a recruiter now." She paused, fidgeting with the glass between her fingers before continuing. "Danny—that's my brother —picked Grace up from school for me that day. He helps me a lot."

Drew nodded, but he still needed to know the answer to the most important question. "And your husband?"

A shaky hand lifted the glass to her lips and she took a longer sip this time. "Jackson."

Not a denial. The world suddenly tipped on its axis, and he grabbed onto the edge of the table until the dizziness in his head passed. He broke out in a cold sweat as the realization hit him that she did have a husband. "Jackson is your husband?" he prodded, needing to know the answer but fearing it all the same.

She nodded and then confirmed his worst fear. "Yes, he was my husband."

Wait, past tense? His pulse quickened at the revelation.

H annah knew from Drew's body language and the hope gleaming in his eye that he believed she and Jackson had gotten divorced. After all, that was the natural conclusion when one heard someone *was* their husband. If only things were that black and white.

Taking a deep breath to steady her nerves, she continued. "Jackson and Danny were best friends growing up. Danny's four years older than me, and somewhere around the time I turned fifteen, I fell madly in love with Jackson."

Her eyes crinkled as she remembered him. She had been a gangly teenager following him around like a puppy, and he had done everything he could to avoid her.

Drew drummed his fingertips restlessly on the tabletop, not so subtly prompting her to continue. She raised a brow as she stared at them pointedly, and his fingers stilled instantly.

"After high school, both boys joined the army. They did basic together and somehow ended up deployed overseas. It was two years before either of them returned home again."

She was quiet for a moment as she recalled that visit. Both men had come home to surprise her for her high school graduation. No one had known they were coming, but the best gift had been jumping into Jackson's arms, his face filled with surprise that she was no longer a little girl. When he'd hugged her back, it had been filled with the promise of so much more.

"The boys stayed home for three weeks. Jackson and I spent almost every moment of that time together. By the time he left, we realized we were madly in love with each other."

She glanced up at Drew then to try and gauge his reaction to her proclamation. His face was void of emotion, but his hands were clenched into tight fists on the table. She picked up the pace.

"Of course, both the boys had to go back. Jackson came back twice in the next year, and during the second visit, we eloped. I was only nineteen years old. My parents weren't thrilled, but Jackson and I knew what we wanted."

Hannah's chest rose as she inhaled deeply and then let out a long sigh. "He was gone for almost a year before coming home on leave again."

She'd moved into a little apartment and tried making it into a home for them. She had been so young. And so lonely. Her parents had died six months after her wedding, her sister was busy starting her own family, and her brother, of course, was overseas too. She hadn't heard from Jackson very often, so it had been hard. When he'd finally gotten leave and stayed with her for a whole month, it had been absolutely perfect. It had been what she'd thought their life was supposed to be like.

"After a month, he had to go back again. But then, about six weeks after he left, I found out I was pregnant."

Hannah looked down and placed a hand over her stomach as she remembered. "He came home two days before I had Grace. He was home for two weeks. He promised me that after that tour, he would come home for good so we could be together as a family."

She looked up and smiled sadly at Drew. He had relaxed his fists, but he kept wiping his palms against his thighs every few seconds.

"We didn't see him again for ten months. His Humvee struck an IED. His wounds were minor, though, and not the reason he came home. Several of the men on the truck died and another was transported here back to the states for recovery. He came for their funerals. He was so angry. I almost didn't recognize him. He didn't understand how he could have come out of the accident with barely a scratch when his friends had died."

He'd spent nearly every day at the hospital with his friend. She'd barely seen him. When she had, he wouldn't look her in the eye. She'd known. She shook her head in anger then, her voice becoming strained as she forced herself to finish.

"Before he even told me, I knew he had re-upped for another tour. When I finally confronted him, he told me he had to go back to honor those he had lost. He couldn't stay here. He said he had to make things right. It was as if Grace and I didn't exist for him anymore. I begged and pleaded with him not to go. Tried to tell him that God had given him another chance so he could be here with us. Even my brother, who was home then, tried to reason with him. But it didn't matter. He couldn't see beyond his grief."

She flinched when Drew's hands wrapped around hers. "Hannah, you can stop if you need to. It's enough. It's obvious this is painful for you."

"No, just let me finish. I want you to know. To understand."

His grip loosened, his hands leaving hers as he leaned back in his chair, nodding for her to continue. She rushed her next words, just wanting to get them out and over with. It still wasn't easy for her to say them out loud.

"He went back. He left us." Her eyes squeezed shut for a moment, a ragged breath leaving her before the next words fell like a brick. "And three months later, he was dead." She dragged her eyes up to meet his, sadness rimming their edges. "I'm still not sure exactly what happened. No one really ever wants to tell us at home the whole truth. His commanding officer said he was on patrol in a small town, performing reconnaissance. They met with resistance and he was shot and killed."

She shrugged, her lips turned down in a frown. "All I know is that I never got to see him again because I was advised to have a closed-casket funeral."

She was proud of herself for keeping her voice steady. She looked up to meet Drew's gaze. His eyes were closed tight.

"Drew?" She touched him on the shoulder. His eyes opened slowly.

"I'm so, so sorry, Hannah."

"There's more though. And this is the part that I'm not proud of." His face remained neutral, not giving away anything he was feeling.

"You've told me enough. I don't need to know anymore. I can't imagine what you must have gone through, that loss and trying to raise a little girl by yourself ."

"But I want you to know. As much as I'm ashamed and afraid to tell you, I want you to know it all. Then maybe I can make you understand why I can't be with you."

All the sympathy he had felt was suddenly washed away in a wave of frustration. "Yes, please tell me then. Because I don't understand why you can't be with me if you aren't married anymore."

Hannah wrung her hands in her lap, nodding as she continued. "After the funeral, which I barely remember, I didn't know what to do or how to cope. I felt so angry, and so empty. I couldn't believe I would never get to talk to Jackson again. Or that Grace would never get to know how wonderful her father was. My brother came and stayed in our little apartment with us. He tried so hard to help. But I couldn't look at him, or even at Grace, without seeing Jackson."

There was a pause as her eyes met his. He nodded. "Go on."

Fidgeting in her chair, she continued. "So, I disappeared. I just didn't come home one day. I went to a bar and started drinking. And I didn't stop for two months. I went home with anyone who would have me, as long as it meant I didn't have to go home. And I did drugs. Anything that would keep me in a permanent haze so I wouldn't have to feel. I was walking a tightrope and barely hanging on. But the thing was, at the time, I didn't care. If I had fallen, I wouldn't have cared one little bit."

He understood now why she had been nervous, but it was still a shock to hear about her drug abuse and sexual oblivion. "You wanted to join Jackson." It was a statement. He didn't need her to confirm it, but she nodded anyway, her cheeks reddening.

"After about three months of this, my sister Tammy found me and dragged me kicking and screaming into a mental health center. I wanted to kill her. But of course, she did the right thing. After another month of dealing with my anger and my loss, I went home. And I promised myself that from that point on, everything I ever did would be for me and Grace. I will never let myself be vulnerable like that again. Ever."

Hannah's timid eyes met his. He should try to be kind, but anger and confusion clouded his judgment, his voice coming out harsh.

"I don't understand. Are you an alcoholic? An addict?"

"No, I used it as a crutch to hide from my real problem. Although I never did drugs before Jackson's death. And I haven't touched them since I got help. I just used whatever was handy to make me forget about my real life. I just wanted to be numb. You've seen me drink socially. I can take it or leave it. But it's not something that I need. If that makes any sense at all."

"I don't know if it makes any sense. I've seen you drink, and I do think you may have a problem knowing what your limits are."

She shifted in her seat and her face turned a light shade of pink. She uncrossed her legs and made a move to stand, but Drew stopped her with a hand on her arm.

"Stay. I'm sorry if I'm making you uncomfortable. I'm just trying to understand."

Her body relaxed back in the chair and she folded her hands in her lap. "This is uncomfortable. I basically just told you I whored myself to forget my dead husband. It's not my proudest moment."

He winced. "Ouch. That's being a little harsh."

She shrugged. "It is what it is. I'm not going to pretend otherwise."

He gazed at her a moment, watching her chest rise and fall quickly, waiting for her breathing to slow before continuing. "I'm sorry your husband died, and I'm even sorrier that you had to go through so much pain because of it, but I'm not going to let you push me away because you're afraid to get hurt again. That's not living."

"But I am living. I'm living a life that I chose for myself. It's safe. Grace is happy. I'm happy."

He stood up then and walked over to one of the full-length windows, shoving his hands in the pockets of his jeans before closing his eyes and lifting his face into the sun.

"Come here and stand next to me."

Her clothes rustled as she rose from the chair and then her boots tapped over to him. He peeked at her through one eye before turning back toward the window.

"Close your eyes."

He couldn't be sure she was following his commands, but she wasn't arguing or questioning him, so he trusted she had complied.

"Do you feel it, Hannah?"

"Feel what?" He could hear the confusion in her voice.

"The sun. The heat. Do you feel it?" He chuckled at her continued stubbornness.

"Umm, yes. I can feel it."

He opened his eyes and watched her nod. "Tell me what you feel."

She raised her head up higher to the light, her eyes scrunching up a bit more tightly. "It's warm, and bright on my lids. My skin feels lighter somehow."

"Keep your eyes closed."

Drew walked away from her and flipped a switch, closing the motorized blinds. The room grew darker and the warmth from the sun faded.

"Drew?"

He stepped up behind her and whispered in her ear. "Don't open your eyes yet. Just tell me what you feel now."

"Cooler. Darker."

"Is it better?" He asked softly.

"Better than what?"

"Than the sun and light you felt?"

She opened her eyes and spun around, coming face to face with him. Instead of stepping back, he leaned down and grasped her arms gently. "To me, you are the sun and the light. You brought warmth into my life again. And I think I did that for you as well. I know it feels safer to stay inside where you can hide in the shadows, but is that really living?"

His hands moved up her arms to grasp her more tightly around the shoulders, his tone pleading. "Let me show you the light again. Even if it's one ray at a time, don't you want to feel that warmth again? Don't you want to share that with your daughter?"

She bit her lower lip and responded shakily, "I'm scared. So scared, Drew. I can't go through that kind of pain again and I think-" She shook her head as her eyes locked on his. "I think being with you could break me."

"I'm scared too. But I'm more scared of not seeing you again. We can go as slow as you want." He leaned in then and, ever so tenderly, kissed her.

As his lips met hers, she sighed in defeat and returned his kiss. Gently at first, but then she clutched his neck with one hand while the other bunched the fabric of his T-shirt on his chest. His hands left her arms and wound through her hair as he held her fast. She parted her lips and darted her tongue out, swiping it against his mouth, which he gladly opened to her. As their kiss intensified, her body melted into his.

Drew broke the kiss but continued holding her in his arms. Looking down into her eyes, he chuckled. "See? Aren't you already feeling warmer?"

He pressed several more small kisses to her face. "Tell me you'll at least try. Let me see you again."

She nodded once, brought her eyes up to his, and breathed out her response. "Okay."

CHAPTER FOUR

"Okay?" Drew couldn't believe his ears. She was agreeing to see him again.

She nodded shyly. "Yes. I'm terrified, but I'm even more scared of not feeling the way I do again when I'm with you. I'm a mess, Drew."

Instead of speaking, Drew pulled her back to his lips to kissed her with more passion than she could ever remember feeling before. His hands stayed tangled in her hair, but he gently turned her and, using his body, backed her up until she hit the shades covering the window. His body was now flush with hers, his hard length pressing into her.

Her hands wrapped around his neck and shoulders while she hooked one leg around his waist, as if she were trying to fuse herself to him. He released her hair, sliding his hands under her bottom, lifting her, her other leg finding its way around his waist as she locked herself around him.

He rocked his hips into her core. She moaned as her head fell back against the window. He took advantage of her exposed neck and trailed his lips down to her bare shoulder, his hand pulling her shirt down further, his lips skimming the tops of her breasts.

Her hardened nipples peaked beneath her shirt, and he wanted nothing more than to take one into his mouth and suck. Grabbing her firmly around the waist, he spun and strode to the living room. "Hold on, Hannah."

Her grip around his neck tightened before he lowered himself into a seated position on the couch, her legs straddling his hips. They looked at each other for only a moment before their lips crashed together once again. Their tongues danced in a swirl of insatiable desire. He grabbed a handful of her hair, pulling her head back to expose her neck. Hannah gasped in surprise, but then moaned in approval when he ran his tongue up her neck to her lips again, nipping the bottom one gently.

Keeping her hair fisted in one hand, he used the other to pull her shirt down below her breast. *No bra?* "Well, aren't you a wicked little minx."

He grinned wantonly, not waiting for her to respond as he crushed his mouth down on her nipple. He ran his tongue around and then over the hardened tip before covering it completely and sucking hard. Hannah rose up on her knees, grasping his head to pull his mouth tighter to her while sliding her core up and down against his hard cock.

He let go of her nipple with a small pop. "Fuck," hissed from his lips. "Hannah, you're killing me here."

"But what a way to go, right?" she purred, continuing to rub up and down his shaft as she yanked her shirt over her head. Drew's eyes lit up in approval as she dropped her hands to the hem of his shirt and peeled it off him.

"I want to feel you against me," she urged, leaning forward, wrapping her arms around him.

He buried his face in Hannah's hair and inhaled deeply, savoring the floral smell he had remembered so well.

"God, I missed this smell. Your touch." He stroked her hair and then brought his lips to hers in a scorching kiss.

He rose up off the couch just enough to turn and lower Hannah back down, never breaking contact with her skin. He thrust his hips hard into her center, his cock throbbing through the material of his jeans. He wanted to be inside her, and now. He pulled back, eliciting a moan of protest from Hannah, but when he began to unbutton her jeans, she reached up to do the same to his.

BZZZZZZZ. BZZZZZZZ. Something vibrated under Hannah, and they both froze.

"My phone," Hannah replied, gently pushing Drew back with one hand so she could reach into her back pocket and retrieve it.

Drew sat back on his heels as she looked at her screen, her brows furrowing in question before she answered. "Hey, Tammy. What's up?"

The expression on her face went from mild curiosity to alarm, her head bobbing up and down as she spoke. "Okay." Silence for a moment. "But is she okay?" Her voice was edged with panic now. "All right, all right. I'm downtown so I'll get there as fast as I can."

Hannah hung up, then reached for her shirt, pulling it quickly over her head before standing up. "I have to go. Grace fell off the monkey bars at the playground and cut her head open. Can you have George call me a cab?"

Drew stood up, pulling his shirt back on again as well. "Don't be silly. I'll drive you. Let me just get some shoes on."

Hannah was pulling her jacket on now and pacing at the same time. "Okay, but hurry. She's hurt." A small cry of worry escaped before she clamped her hand over her mouth.

He pulled her into his arms. "Hannah, I'm sure it's going to be okay. Kids fall all the time."

She pushed out of his arms in frustration. "How would you know? Do you have kids? Were you the one sitting here about to fuck someone when your child was bleeding on a playground somewhere?" She pointed a shaking finger back and forth between them, her eyes wild with anger. "This! This is why I can't do this again."

He blew out a slow breath, not wanting to incite her further. She was just scared for her daughter. He walked toward the hallway and opened a closet. He pulled out a pair of sneakers, quickly slid them onto his bare feet and then pulled on a soft-looking leather jacket. He turned to her then and took one of her hands. "Come on. Let's get to her then."

———

J ust a few minutes later, they were pulling out of the hotel parking garage in his Jag. Hannah had sent another text asking Tammy for an update but hadn't received a reply. "Which hospital?"

"The NYU ER on First Avenue. Do you know where it is?"

"I do." He shifted the car into a higher gear and weaved in and out of traffic. He was doing everything he could to get her there as fast as he could, and she was being ungrateful. She placed her hand over his on the gearshift and squeezed. He glanced at her, startled.

"I'm sorry, Drew. I shouldn't have snapped at you like that." She gave him her most apologetic smile.

In turn he pulled her fingers into his and smiled. "I know you're scared. You weren't doing anything wrong though."

She looked down at the hand in her lap, fidgeting with her phone. "It's just that after all the time I wasn't there for her, I make sure I always am now. Then the one time I'm not, something happens."

He frowned. "It's not your fault, Hannah. It's not. Kids play hard and accidents happen. They also bounce back quickly too. This could have happened even if you were right there in the park with her."

"But I wasn't." She shook her head as she repeated herself. "I wasn't."

Drew squeezed her fingers, then let go and pointed out the window. "Look, almost there. It's one block up. I'll drop you off in front and go park the car. Go find Grace and I'll meet you inside."

She reared back. "You're coming in?"

He tilted his head as he pulled up in front of the hospital. "Yes, of course. I want to make sure your daughter's okay. That you're both okay."

She blew out a deep breath, trying to expel some of the nerves coursing through her veins. "I'd rather you didn't. I'll call you later. Tammy can give me a ride home."

Drew shook his head, then nodded, his lips pursed. "Okay, fine."

"Thank you for the ride and for understanding. I'll call you." She opened the door, stepped out of the car and hurried through the entrance. After a brief exchange of information with an attendant at the front desk and the signing of what seemed like a hundred insurance forms, she was finally brought down to Grace's exam room.

Instead of the scared, crying child she had been expecting, Grace was sitting up in bed, a bandage on her forehead, a grape Popsicle clutched between her fingers. Tammy was sitting on the bed with Grace, her back to the door. From the doorway, she watched her daughter for a moment to make sure she really was okay, then walked in.

"Hey, peanut. You doing okay?"

Grace held her arms out as soon as she saw her mom. "Momma!"

Hannah sat on the bed and pulled her daughter into a tight embrace, kissing the top of her little fluffy head at least six times before letting go. "Hi, baby. How's your head?"

She stroked Grace's hair away from her face and touched her lightly on the skin below the bandage. She turned to Tammy then. "What happened? What did the doctor say?"

"This doctor says she's going to be just fine," said a male voice behind her. A middle-aged man with a shiny bald head came into the room and extended his hand. "Mom, I presume? I'm Dr. Brothers."

Hannah took his hand and shook it. "Yes, hello. I'm Hannah, Grace's mom. She's going to be okay?"

The doctor nodded and smiled warmly. "Yep, this little lady is going to be just fine."

He walked over to Grace then and tickled the bottom of her

foot, making her squirm and drip some of her Popsicle onto the bedding. He turned back to Hannah. "We put a couple butterfly strips on her forehead, but the cut wasn't so deep that it required stitches. No loss of consciousness and very little swelling, so I don't see any reason to worry about a concussion. She's got a good hard head on her."

Hannah smiled in relief. "Oh, thank god. And thank you, Doctor."

"Just doing my job. The nurse will come by in a few minutes to sign you out so you can take her home."

"Thank you again." Hannah shook his hand again before he left the room.

Tammy got up off the bed and pulled Hannah into a hug. "I'm so, so sorry. I was standing right there, helping Emma climb up the jungle gym to sit with Grace. She reached down to grab Emma's hand and lost her grip and fell right through the middle of the bars. She smacked her head on one of the bars going down."

Hannah pulled away from her sister and patted her on the arm in reassurance. "It's okay. It was an accident. And she's fine. I trust you with Grace's life."

Tammy's eyes moved to the doorway and grew a bit wider. Hannah twisted around to see what had her sister's attention. Drew was standing in the doorway, a pink, stuffed teddy bear in hand.

"What are you doing here?" she hissed, too low for Grace to hear.

Instead of answering, Drew nodded at Tammy and extended his free hand to her.

"Andrew Sapphire. Nice to meet you."

Tammy looked back and forth between them before finally placing her hand in his, practically swooning as she responded. "Hi. Tammy, Hannah's big sister."

"Yes, she's told me about you. Very nice to meet you." He gently extracted his hand from hers.

Tammy turned to Hannah, keeping her back to Drew. Her eyes

were wide in astonishment as she mouthed silently, "Oh my god!" Then in a normal voice, "Okay, well, now that you're here, Hannah, I'm going to go ahead and head home. I had one of the other moms take Emma for me so I still need to go and pick her up."

She gave Grace a big kiss and hug and did the same to Hannah before walking past Drew. "Nice to meet you, Andrew."

Drew walked further into the room as she passed. "You as well."

He squeezed Hannah's arm and tilted his head toward the bed in question before moving any closer. "Is she okay?"

"She is. Just a bad cut. No concussion."

He raised the stuffed animal in his hands slightly. "Is it okay if I give her the bear?"

She stared down at the bear in his hand a moment before nodding, silently wondering how this was going to go. She had never introduced any other men to Grace. Ever.

Drew took a couple steps closer to the bed and then knelt down so he was face to face with Hannah's daughter. "You must be Grace."

Grace bit her lower lip and lowered her eyes, nodding up and down.

"My name is Drew. I'm a friend of your mom's. I heard you had quite a fall and hurt your head."

Again, Grace just nodded up and down. Drew brought the teddy bear up and placed it on the bed next to Grace. "Well, the nice lady at the gift store said this teddy bear is so soft and cuddly it's guaranteed to make you feel better."

Grace looked up at Hannah in silent question. Hannah nodded. "It's okay, Gracie. You can take the bear."

Grace finally released her lower lip from her teeth and tentatively reached for the teddy bear Drew offered. She pulled it into her arms, a smile breaking wide across her little face. "Thank you, Mr. Drew."

He smiled warmly at her, patted her hand and then stood up. "You are so very welcome. I hope you feel better really soon."

"What's her name?"

Drew tilted his head, surprise on his face. "Whose name, honey?"

"The bear. She has to have a name."

Drew scratched the scruff on his chin. She couldn't help enjoying the obviously new territory he had ventured into. "Oh. Hmm, I guess we need to give her one, eh? Any ideas?"

Her daughter stroked the bear's soft fur and then smiled brightly. "How about Pinky?"

"I think Pinky is perfect."

Right at that moment, the nurse came in carrying the discharge paperwork. "All right, is this little one all ready to go home?"

She and Grace responded in unison, "Yes!"

After all the paperwork was signed and Grace was back in her shoes and jacket, Hannah lifted Grace off the bed and into her arms. Grace clutched the teddy bear fiercely.

"Do you want me to take her for you?" Drew asked.

Hannah smiled appreciatively at him. "No, I've got her. Would you mind walking me out though? I could use some help getting a cab."

"A cab?" His brow furrowed. "Nonsense. Let me take you home. I'll bring the car around."

"But your car is a two-seater." Hannah screeched to a halt. " And oh jeez, I don't have a car seat either."

"Hannah, it will be fine. We're only a few blocks from your place. We'll buckle you both in nice and tight, and I promise I'll drive extra carefully."

She blew her breath out in surrender, her arms already getting tired from holding her daughter. "Okay. But extra careful!"

He reached out and gently ruffled Grace's hair as she started walking again. "I promise. Precious cargo on board. I'll go get the car and meet you at the main entrance, okay?"

She nodded in agreement. "Okay, meet you there."

Ten minutes later, she and Grace were all buckled up in Drew's car as he pulled away from the curb.

"You remember where the flower shop is? Grace and I live upstairs."

"Yes, I know."

Hannah whipped her head around. "You know?"

Drew shifted the car to a lower gear and cleared his throat. "Yes, I know."

Hannah stared at him for a good long time before responding. "I would ask how, but at this point, I really don't think I want to know."

At a red light, Drew turned and looked her directly in the eyes. "It's your fault, you know."

"What's my fault?" Hannah pulled Grace a little tighter into her lap, making sure she was still secure. She was busy having a very serious conversation with Pinky about the other animals she would meet when she got home.

"The reason I couldn't stay away from you."

"What reason was that?"

He closed his eyes for the briefest of moments and inhaled deeply. He opened them again and accelerated, the light green. "Your smile, the way your hair smells, the way you have to turn every conversation into a challenge, the way you respond to me, the way you taste."

His voice trailed off and a small electric shock ran through her body at his admission. She looked at him, her eyes hooded with a new surge of desire. "Oh. I'm sorry then."

This time a wicked smile curved his lips. "I'm not. Not even a little bit."

Her cheeks went crimson as blood rushed through and heated her body. When he darted a glance her way, she widened her eyes and tipped her head at Grace, silently pleading with him to end this conversation. He raised his hand, brushing it lightly over her cheek and then turned his eyes back to the road.

"Here we are, ladies."

Hannah turned forward and realized he had pulled into the alley of the shop.

"Would you like some help in with Grace?"

She shook her head and looked down at her daughter. "No, thank you. I think it's been enough for one day."

His lips pursed, he nodded curtly. "Let me at least help you out of the car."

Before she could answer, he had swung his door open and stepped out. In another moment, her door was open and he was bending down, lifting Grace up and placing her gently on the sidewalk. Hannah stepped quickly out and took hold of Grace's hand.

"Thank you for the ride. And for getting us home."

His hand dragged roughly over the light stubble on his chin, his eyes looking toward the sky before he responded. "Sure, no problem. Can I call you later?"

She looked down at Grace, who was looking up at her curiously, the teddy bear hugged to her chest in her other arm. Grace had to be her priority right now.

"I'll try and call you later tonight after I put Grace down." She started walking toward the door, pulling her daughter gently along. "Thank you again."

"Hannah, wait."

She stopped and turned as Drew closed the gap between them. He reached into the back pocket of his jeans and pulled his wallet out.

"What?" She wasn't sure what he was doing.

He pulled out a white business card and handed it to her. "This has my cell number on it. I'm pretty sure you only have my office number. Or you could have called the hotel, I guess."

"Oh." She took the white card and, without looking at it, slipped it into the front pocket of her jeans. "Okay. Thanks again."

She turned and walked to the door before he could say anything else. His footsteps retreated in the other direction as she pulled her keys out of her jacket pocket and breathed a sigh of relief.

CHAPTER FIVE

D rew twirled the stem of the martini glass in his fingers as he debated whether or not to have another. He was sitting in one of the leather upholstered stools in the bar of his hotel, so it wasn't like he had to get into a car and drive. It was ten p.m. Monday evening and Hannah still hadn't called him.

"Another Hendrick's martini, Mr. Sapphire?" the bartender asked, taking the empty glass from his hands.

"Please." Fuck it. One more isn't going to hurt at this point. The pretty bartender filled a new martini glass with ice to chill it and then poured a healthy amount of gin and vermouth into the shaker. She caught him watching her as she shook the container. She smiled shyly, her cheeks blushing a light pink, before she looked away to finish preparing his drink.

She placed a new napkin in front of him before setting the full glass down on it. "Sir."

He raised the glass in a toast before bringing it to his lips for a sip. "Thank you."

The bartender's eyes followed the glass to his mouth and stayed there until he lowered it back to the bar. She raised her gaze again to meet his stare.

"Can I get you anything else, sir?" Her voice was husky, lower than before.

Her question implied more than a polite inquiry for a dish of nuts. She would happily accompany him to his room and serve him anything he wanted if he asked. And three months ago he probably would have done just that. She was attractive and attentive, and best of all, the way she called him "sir" suggested she would be more than submissive.

"No, thank you." He smiled kindly to take the sting out of his rejection. The only person he wanted now was Hannah. No one else was even remotely tempting. But after two days with no phone call, it looked like she didn't fucking want him.

The bartender nodded. "Just let me know if you need anything else." She turned and walked to the other end of the bar to tend to another patron.

Drew raised the glass to his mouth. Just as he was about to take a large swig, someone slapped him on the shoulder and sat down beside him, sloshing some of the gin out of the glass and onto the bar. He spun to give the person a piece of his mind, then stopped abruptly.

"Son." His father made himself comfortable on the stool next to him and raised his hand to get the bartender's attention.

"Dad." Drew brought the glass up again and this time managed to take that large swig.

"Give me three fingers of the Talisker, straight up please."

The bartender poured the scotch and had it sitting in front of his father on a fresh napkin in less than thirty seconds. She was good. He picked it up and sniffed the warm, brown liquid before taking a drink.

"What are you doing here this late?" Drew asked as his father sipped his scotch.

"Business." There was an edge to his voice.

His father often worked late into the night at their various hotels to avoid going home before his mother went to bed. His father loved his mother. And she loved him. The loyalty Gavin and Caroline Sapphire still showed each other more than proved that to him. But after his sister had died, something between them had died too. His mother could never seem to pull herself completely out of her grief, and his father escaped in his work instead of trying to help her.

"Will we see you at the house for dinner on Thursday? I believe Benjamin may actually join us."

"I'm not sure yet. I may have other plans."

His father's face pinched in anger. "Your mother will be disappointed." His father sighed. They tried to have a family dinner once a week, one of the only times his mother seemed fairly happy.

"I should know better by tomorrow. But if I can't make it, I'll call and set up a lunch date with her."

His father nodded. "I'm sure she'd like that." He brought the glass up, drained the rest of his scotch and placed it back on the bar before standing up. "Well, Carl's waiting with the car. I saw you sitting here and just wanted to say hello."

Drew raised himself up off the barstool and faced his father. "Send Mom my love."

"Jesus, what happened to your eye!" His father reached out and touched the left side of Drew's face. That side must have been hidden when he'd been sitting at the bar. Drew pulled away from his father's hand and grinned.

"Benny took me boxing. I lost."

"Is this why you cancelled our meeting the other day?"

Drew nodded in response.

"God damn Benjamin." His father laughed and shook his head in dismay. "He always loved to give you a beating."

Drew shrugged. "Nah, it's all good. It wasn't Benny. I was in the ring with some other guy and he was just better."

His father touched the side of Drew's face again, gently this time, and then wrapped one arm around his shoulder, clapping him on the back before turning away. "Good night, Andrew."

"Good night, Dad." His father walked out of the low-lit lounge into the lobby, toward the front doors. Drew picked up his martini glass, finished what was left and motioned to the bartender that he was leaving.

After signing the slip and leaving a fifty-dollar tip, he headed up to his suite. It was a good thing he didn't have Hannah's cell number or he'd be drunk dialing it right now. Tomorrow. Tomorrow he was going to talk to her. Even if he had to go to her again.

H annah's heart leapt into her throat as she pulled into the alley. Drew stood in front of the shop doorway. She had a feeling he would show up sooner or later. She'd just hoped it would be later, like at least a week later, so she had more time to build up some resistance to his charm. She shut the engine off, steeling herself to defend her decision not to see him.

She stepped out. It was freezing. How could he stand there in just a sweatshirt and sweats as the wind whipped around him? He pushed his hood off his head as she approached.

"You didn't call." His voice was low but not demanding.

She unlocked the metal casing and then the interior door. "Come in, Drew. It's cold."

The bell above the door tinkled, announcing their arrival as they stepped inside the warmth of the shop. She walked to the back and into the work room, taking her jacket off as she went. She was trying to appear confident, but if she started speaking, her voice was going to wobble. She just wanted another minute to gather her thoughts. She hung up her coat, then pulled a stool out from under the table and sat on it.

Drew pulled one out to her right and sat on it, facing her. "You didn't call."

She stood up abruptly. "Do you want some water? You ran here, I assume?" Her eyes scanned up and down his athletically dressed form.

"I don't want any water. Just tell me why you haven't called."

She lowered herself back onto the stool and began fidgeting with some ribbon lying on the table.

"You said you would try." He reached across the table and pulled the ribbon from her fingers.

She looked up at him finally. "That was before."

"Before what?" His forehead creased.

"Before Grace got hurt—while I was about to have sex with you! I made a promise to myself that my daughter would always come first. And the first time I'm with you, the first time, something happens to her. It's a sign."

"It's a sign?" He didn't bother to hide his disbelief.

"Call it whatever you want. It was a reminder to me about what my priorities need to be."

His hand slammed on the table, making her jump. "Jesus fucking Christ, Hannah! Really? Do you think for one second I would ask you to ever turn your back on your child or your responsibilities to her? Are you really going to try and hide behind that excuse?"

"Don't you yell at me! You have no idea what it's like to have to raise a child on your own. Especially after the things I did to her. I won't desert her like that again!" She lowered the finger she had been pointing at him, hiding her shaking hand. Before it hit the table, he grabbed it between his two palms.

"You didn't do anything wrong. There's a big difference between leaving your child in someone else's care when an accident happens and deserting her. I can see what a good mother you are. You don't have to keep punishing yourself to prove that."

His voice was as gentle as his caresses. "I'm not asking you to turn your back on Grace, nor would I ever. I'm just asking you to make a little room for me. To see if maybe we have a chance. And 'we' means all three of us, not just you and me. I understand that."

"I don't think you understand how hard this really is for me. There's never been another man in my daughter's life because I've never let another man in my life. This is huge for me. And I asked you not to come into the hospital, and then you did, further complicating things and not respecting what I asked. That was about my daughter. Not about me."

Deflated, Drew lowered his head. "I know. I'm sorry. I realized that after the fact. I acted on impulse and that was stupid of me. I should have known better. I only wanted to make sure you were okay. That your daughter was okay."

"I appreciate that, but I've been taking care of myself and her for a very long time now. If I needed your help, I would have asked."

He met her eyes with an apologetic frown. "It won't happen again."

She shook her head in doubt. "I wish I could believe that. You like control. Giving that up to someone isn't in your nature."

"In the bedroom." He glowered back. "Not over your life. Not over your child. I know where the line is. I won't cross it again. Give me another chance. Give us another chance. Please." He brought her hand to his lips and kissed the fingertips gently. "Please."

She liked him. She wanted him. She wasn't going to lie to herself about that. And when he touched her like this, even just small kisses to her fingers, she remembered what it felt like to be held by him. But how did she balance that and what was right for her daughter?

As if he could read her mind, he spoke again. "What if the three of us have dinner so I can meet your daughter properly?"

Her heart finally gave in, but it needed to find some common ground with her head. "Okay, dinner. But it has to be at my place. I think it will be easier for Grace if she's in her own environment."

A smile broke across his face. "Your place is perfect. Is tonight too soon?"

She laughed despite herself. "Now who's anxious? Tonight is actually good. Besides, I'm making your favorite."

He cocked his head. "My favorite?"

She grinned. "Yep. Grilled cheese and tomato soup."

Drew broke into a wide grin as well, obviously remembering with fondness the very same lunch they had shared together after their first time in the playroom. "That sounds perfect."

"Okay, come by around six."

CHAPTER SIX

A t precisely six p.m., Drew rang the doorbell and waited. Within moments, the door swung open and Hannah stood before him. She was dressed in a pair of black leggings and an over-sized long-sleeved T-shirt, her hair up in a ponytail. She looked simple, but beautiful as always.

"Hi! Come in! It's so cold out there." She shut the door behind him.

He bent and kissed her on the cheek. "Hi. Is it okay that I'm nervous?"

"Yep, 'cause I am too." She grinned up at him and then looked down at his hands. "Whatcha got there?"

"Oh! It's cupcakes. Since getting you flowers is out, I got a dozen of these instead. In all flavors, of course, because I didn't know what you girls liked."

He laughed when she jumped up and down and clapped her hands like a little kid. *Thank god I took Felicia's suggestion.*

"Oh this is perfect! We love cupcakes!" She grabbed the box from his hands and started up the steps. "Come on, let me intro-duce you to Grace again and show you our home."

At the top of the stairs, she showed him where he could hang his coat. As he took it off and hung it on one of the proffered hooks, he looked around and absorbed the essence of her home. Grace came running in, stopping in her tracks when she saw Drew.

"Honey, do you remember Mommy's friend Drew from the hospital?"

Grace kept her eyes glued on him as she inched her way to her mother's side, wrapping her little arms around her leg once she was there.

Drew bent down to eye level and smiled warmly. "Hey, Gracie. How's your head doing?" He pointed to the small teal Band-Aid on her forehead.

She rubbed her forehead with little fingers until she found it, then shrugged her shoulders. "It's okay now. Mommy says I only have to wear the Band-Aid one more day."

She let go of her mother's leg then and walked closer to him. "Your face has prickles!" she said, brushing her hands back and forth against Drew's cheeks.

He couldn't help but grin broadly at her assessment of his unshaven face. "Yep, I guess it does."

Hannah stared down at them.

"What?" His brows raising.

"Nothing." She lifted a hand to her face in an attempt to hide her turned up mouth, turning quickly. "Come on, I'll show you the rest of the place."

He followed her and Grace down a short hallway that opened up into a large eat-in kitchen. She put the cupcakes down and then swung around in a little circle with open arms. "Welcome to my kitchen."

Grace twirled, mimicking her mother and echoing, "Welcome to my kitchen." She giggled freely as she continued to spin.

"All right, little monkey, not too much." Hannah placed her hands gently on Grace's shoulders to stop her from spinning. "We don't want you to knock your head again."

"Okay, Mommy." She grinned widely. "Can I go watch TV?"

"Sure, sweetie, go ahead."

They both watched as Grace danced her way out of the room

through an open arch into the living room. Drew walked slowly around the kitchen, taking in everything. Squiggly, colorfully lined drawings hung on the fridge, a box of crayons and a Cinderella coloring book lay open on the table, a pink cup sat in the strainer, and a pile of unopened mail lay next to it.

"Sorry, it's a bit messy. I don't usually get time to pick things up until after I put Gracie to bed." She shook her head. "If you had asked me this morning, I definitely wouldn't have said you'd be standing in my kitchen by nightfall."

He took another step closer, laying his hand against her cheek. "Me either, but I'm really glad I'm here."

There was a moment's pause between them before she pulled away. "Let me show you the rest."

She brought him through the arched doorway into the large living space. Grace was lying on a purple velvet beanbag, watching cartoons in front of the TV. A large, dark gray, wrap-around couch took up part of the space. End tables, lamps and several large bookcases took up the rest. The bookcases were filled with picture frames and books. So many pictures of Grace from an infant till now decorated lined the shelves.

One picture was of Hannah. She was wearing a beautiful white sundress and had flowers in her hair. She stood in profile, holding the hand of another man, looking directly at him, sunlight spilling around them. His breath caught, surprise at seeing her looking at another man with so much love and devotion.

He started at her hand on his arm. "That was my wedding day. That's Jackson."

"It's a beautiful picture." He didn't want to be jealous of a ghost, but he was. And he was a total prick for feeling that way. The guy had died for his country.

"Come on, I'll show you upstairs."

He followed Hannah out a doorway off the living room and up another set of stairs. At the top were Grace's bedroom, a full-sized bath and another smaller bedroom.

"Is this your room?" It was pretty sparse. Just a full-sized bed covered in a simple quilt and a bureau with a few items on top.

"No, this is for Danny when he crashes here. My room is downstairs. Come, I'll show you."

She turned and retraced their steps back through the kitchen and out across the hall. She stopped at a set of French doors, turning the handle of one and pushing it open.

"I think this was actually supposed to be the dining room, but I made it into a bedroom so Danny could have the extra one upstairs."

He walked in and was immediately assaulted with her scent: roses and lilies and tulips and jasmine. The room was quintessentially female. A soft white comforter covered a large bed, and yellow and pink throw pillows filled one side of the room. A long dresser up against another wall was covered with loose jewelry, pictures of Grace, perfume bottles and makeup. A white, fluffy rug lay in the center of the hardwood floor, and a soft gray chair sat in a corner, discarded clothing strewn across it.

"Sorry, it's a mess. Like I said, I wasn't expecting company." She paced in place, her cheeks turning a light pink.

"I love it. I love your home. It's lived in, filled with love." He gathered her into his arms and rested his forehead against hers. "You've made a wonderful life here for you both. Thank you for sharing this with me."

"You're welcome."

He ran his hand up her back and her neck before grasping her face gently, bringing his lips to hers. Their breath became one as their lips fused together, their bodies pulling closer to one another. He walked her backward until she hit the door, making it bang against the bedroom wall, but he didn't stop until his body was caging hers.

He tore his lips from hers and brought them to her ear, tracing his tongue around its edges, then blowing lightly. She shivered against him.

"I can't get enough of you, Hannah. Being this close to you is killing me."

She turned her mouth to his and caught his lips in a biting kiss before pushing him away. She was breathing hard and her face was pink. "I know but we have to stop." She nodded toward the living room. "Grace."

Drew nodded in understanding, trying to still some of the desire racing through him. "Maybe I should go?"

Hannah shook her head. "No. No, stay. Please. I'm going to make dinner for us and then put Gracie to bed. We can spend some time together. Okay?"

Drew nodded and was surprised to feel relief that she wanted him to stay.

Hannah could hear Drew washing up the last of the dishes as she pulled Grace out of the tub and wrapped a towel around her little pink body. She had a gorgeous, billionaire dominant down in her kitchen, cleaning up her soup and sandwich dishes. *How in the fuck did I get here?*

She dried Grace off and quickly covered her in baby lotion before pulling her favorite Disney princess nightgown over her damp curls. "Okay, monkey, hop up in bed and I'll read you a story."

Grace climbed up in the bed and under her covers. "Mommy, is Mr. Drew staying at our house tonight?"

Hannah froze. *Shit. How do I answer this question?* "Why would you think that, sweetie?"

"Cause when Uncle Danny stays for dinner, he sleeps over."

She smiled down at Grace. "Well, I think Mr. Drew will be going home in a little while. He just wanted to have dinner with us. Okay?"

Grace yawned and smiled. "Okay. Can we read Cinderella tonight?"

"Again? Aren't you tired of that one?"

"Never!" Grace clapped her hands.

Hannah chuckled and sat down on the bed, cuddling up next to Grace. "Alrighty then, Cinderella it is. Once upon a time . . ."

Ten minutes later, Grace's eyes were closed and she was snoring softly. Hannah tucked her in, turned off her light, shut the door behind her and made her way downstairs. She found Drew sitting on the couch in the living room, a glass of water in hand and another waiting for her on the coffee table.

She reached for it as she sat next to him. "I'm surprised you're still here."

He tilted his head. "Really, why?"

She laughed dryly. "It's a lot of simple domestic bliss I've thrown at you tonight. Not exactly what our relationship was founded on."

He shook his head and blew out a slow breath. "I'm not going to lie. It's a little strange. But being here with you, seeing the real you is exactly what I asked for."

"And you're not ready to run for the hills yet? I mean, I have a child. You see how much of my life is about her. Do you understand that now?"

He brushed her cheek before taking her hand in his. "I have loved seeing this side of you. If this is going to work between us, I need to get to know all of you, and Grace is a part of that. From what I've seen so far, you seem like an incredible mother. But you are so much more than just a mother, Hannah. I've seen the other side of that. The side of you that comes alive under my touch. The side of you that is hungry to be loved and to be seen as a woman too. I'm hoping you'll allow yourself to be both."

She took a drink of her water, trying to quench some of the fire his words sparked. "I'm trying, Drew. I just don't want to get lost in this. And you are so much more."

"So much more?" His head cocked in confusion.

"More man, more money, more beautiful, more dominant, more everything than I've ever experienced before. It's a lot."

He put his glass down on the table and slid closer to her. "It doesn't have to be. It can be a little or a lot, really slow or really fast. I don't care. I just want to be with you. Whatever makes you feel good."

Her head fell back as she laughed. "That's just it. Everything you do makes me feel good. Too good. I don't want to get lost in that and forget everything else."

"Would that be a bad thing?"

She looked down at the water in her glass and then up at him. "It could be. That's what I'm afraid of. I've done it before. Of course, under different circumstances. But what if things really work out between us and I give you everything I have, and then you decide you don't want it anymore? That loss I felt when Jackson died, I can't go through that again. I can't. And I can't risk breaking Grace's heart either."

"This isn't something I thought I'd ever want again. And I definitely didn't factor a child into things. Being a member at the club gave me what I needed and what I thought I wanted. But then you walked up on that stage, and everything changed for me."

She frowned in realization. "I guess it changed everything for me too."

"I suppose we both got a little more than we expected, huh?"

She nodded, chuckling. "Speaking of unexpected. You were really good with Grace tonight. Do you have nieces or nephews?"

He shook his head. "No. It's just Benny and me and he hasn't ever married. And I don't think he has any kids that I know of."

He laughed at his own joke before continuing. "But you know about my sister Lizzie. She was five years younger than me. I loved being her big brother. Gracie reminds me of her in a funny way. Not in looks, but in the sweet, innocent way she does things. I remember being twelve or thirteen and how Lizzie would follow me around everywhere."

Drew was silent for a minute, lost in thought. She went in an entirely different direction with her next question. "What about the other stuff?" Her cheeks turned pink. *Smooth, Hannah.*

"Other stuff? Which stuff?"

"Well, we met at an auction where you bought me for your sexual pleasure. You are a Dominant. What about that part of things?"

Drew ran a hand through his hair, then scratched at the stubble on his chin. Someone was nervous. "Well, I guess that depends on you. You know what I like. But having you is more important to me than anything else right now."

"Right now?"

He looked directly at her, his tone more serious than she'd heard it all night. "Yes, right now. I'm only thinking about right now. I'm not sure about tomorrow, next week or even next month. But right now, I know what I want is you."

"Are you still going to the club?" she whispered, afraid of what his answer might be.

He flinched. "Is that what you're worried about?"

She shrugged. "Well, you're a man. You have needs. And it's been months since you and I . . ."

He leaned forward, his eyes growing darker, his voice low as he responded, "There's been no one since you."

"Oh" slipped from between her lips. "Did you quit?"

He shrugged. "Why would I go back?"

She stared at him in quiet disbelief as his response sunk in. He broke the silence for them. "Why did you join the club? You said it was a job to you and you needed the money, but not just anyone can become part of that lifestyle."

"I wanted to buy this shop and I needed the money."

"But I was your first auction. I know how much a shop like this costs and I certainly didn't pay that much for you." A sly grin fell across his lips.

"Well, no, of course not. Things changed after that weekend. I thought I could have sex without the emotion, but I was wrong. So, I quit." She shrugged, trying to end the topic, but Drew persisted.

"What made you think you could do the job? Have sex with strangers. Without any emotion."

"I guess I have to go back to the beginning to explain."

"Okay."

"I've worked at the shop for several years. We're lucky enough to have some very good clients. You remember Mr. and Mrs. Downing from the ball, right?"

His eyebrows rose. "Harold? Yes. I wondered how you knew him."

"Would you believe he comes in every week and personally picks out flowers for his wife?" She smiled warmly. "Anyway, Baton Timide is, well, was one of our biggest clients. We delivered flowers there three times a week. One day I made the delivery and Domme Maria saw me."

Hannah looked at him and quirked a brow. "You know how she is: no holds barred. She walked right up to me and told me I was beautiful and asked if I liked women. I started laughing at first, but then she gave me that look. You know the one, right?"

Drew chuckled. "Oh yes, I know that look."

"She sat me down and explained what occurred at Baton Timide and told me if I ever wanted a job, to come back and see her. I didn't take her seriously of course. Until I needed money."

"Just like that?"

"No, not just like that." She scoffed. "I'm twenty-seven. I like sex. I like it a lot. And I always liked it a bit rougher than most. But before I had sex with you, it had been two years. I was looking forward to just having sex, to turning everything off and just doing what I was told. And it was in a safe environment. I thought it could be the best of both worlds: have some fun and make the money I need." She raised her eyes, locking them with his. "But you, I wasn't ready for you. You made me feel so good physically, but when you made my heart start beating again-"

She paused and looked up at him apologetically. "I didn't sign up for that. So, I ran. Just like I always do."

"So, you like it? The sex. The domination." His eyes were dark, a feral gleam in their depths.

"Yes. I like it." Her voice was soft and husky, reacting to the change in his demeanor.

He leaned forward then, grasping her lightly around her neck, and brought his lips to hers in a scorching kiss. This, this part with him was always easy. She opened her lips and welcomed his tongue as it swept across hers, teasing and inviting. Their breath became one as the kiss intensified, his heart thudding against the hand that was now up against his chest.

He pushed her away, panting. "More?"

She tilted her head and in less than a second breathed, "More."

"Will Grace wake up?"

"There's a bell above her door. It jingles if she opens it."

"Good." His eyes darkened. "Go to your room and strip naked. Assume your position. Wait for me."

CHAPTER SEVEN

Drew checked his watch one more time to make sure he had
given Hannah enough time to undress and prepare. He
would have normally made her wait longer to build up the anticipation, but they'd had three long months leading up to this
moment.

The French doors to her bedroom were closed and the
windows curtained, but low light shone under the edge. He turned
the door handles and pushed. He froze and sucked in a breath at
the sight before him: Hannah, naked and on her knees. Her head
was cast downward, her blonde hair spilling over her face and
breasts. Her legs were spread open into a V, and her hands were
lying palms up on top of her thighs.

The sound of her quick breathing and her trembling fingertips
betrayed her nervousness—or her excitement. He stepped into the
room and then turned around to shut the doors behind him.
Before turning back, he pulled his T-shirt over his head, took a
deep breath and tossed it to the floor.

He stepped forward until he was directly in front of her. He
reached down and stroked her hair. He could practically feel her
purr under his touch. *Fuck, she is going to kill me.*

"Hannah, give me your hand." His voice was hoarse with desire. Not lifting her head a fraction, she raised her hand up to him. He took it and placed it over his cock, pressing her hand against it. "Feel how fucking hard you make me."

Her fingers spread around his length and began slowly rubbing up and down. From under her blonde curtain, a breathy reply reached his ears. "Yes, Sir."

He didn't think it was possible, but his cock grew even harder, twitching in his pants. *Jesus fucking Christ.* He brushed her hand aside and unbuttoned his jeans, pushing them down and freeing his cock at the same time. Sweet relief. Until she placed her hand back over his length and continued to rub.

"Look at me," he growled through gritted teeth.

Her gaze met his, her mouth now in perfect alignment with his throbbing cock. Not saying a word and keeping his eyes glued to her face, he fisted his cock and brought it to her lips. A groan escaped him as her pink tongue darted out and licked a drop of pre-cum off the tip of his cock before she opened wide.

Her eyes stayed glued to his as she sucked his cock deep into her mouth, swirling her tongue around it as she went. When she had it in as far as she could take it, she sealed her lips around him and sucked hard. He threw his head back with a loud moan, grasping her hair in both his hands.

She continued to suck as she slid her mouth up and down his cock. Just when he didn't think he could feel any fucking better, she started to hum. The vibration drove straight down his cock to his balls, which drew up tight, more than ready to spring. He hadn't been with anyone since Hannah, so it wasn't going to take long for him to come. Tightening the grasp on her hair, he pulled himself free from her mouth with a loud pop before he could explode.

"Get on the bed. I want you on your hands and knees. Now," he panted.

She was up and on the bed in less than five seconds, her ass facing him. He gripped his cock as he strode over to her and smacked her ass hard with his free hand. "Shoulders down on the bed. I want your ass in the air."

Hannah let out a small yelp of surprise with the smack but instantly complied and fell onto her shoulders, her ass straight up. He rubbed his cock with one hand and traced the outline his palm had left on her ass with the other.

"Jesus, Hannah, your ass is so fucking beautiful." He fondled her ass with one hand while the other stroked his cock. His balls started to tighten and he stepped closer, palming her ass firmly as he exploded onto it with a loud groan. As the last drop fell from his softening cock, he dropped to his knees before he could fall and pushed Hannah's legs farther apart. "Don't move."

"Yes, Sir."

He grinned like the Cheshire Cat at her compliance. He brought his nose between her legs and inhaled deeply, taking in every ounce of her essence, and then ran his tongue up the inside of her thigh. Wetness had dripped down from her core onto her leg. He lapped at it with two long strokes before moving to her center, dragging his tongue down in one long swipe.

She arched her back lower and pushed herself into him, but instead of punishing her, he drove his tongue into her pussy. She let out a soft groan, then his name on her breath. "Oh, Drew."

"You're so fucking wet." Not waiting for or wanting an answer from her, he continued tonguing her center. He started to get hard again and moaned at the thought of finally sliding into her again. He skimmed his hand up her ass and began running his thumb around her hole, using his cum as a lubricant. Instead of resisting, she moaned, pushing back into his thumb. His cock was instantly hard.

He trailed his tongue up her pussy, found her clit and pulled into his mouth, sucking hard as he pushed his thumb into her ass.

"Ohhh, please don't stop . . . "

Drew smiled and continued sucking lightly on her clit,

pumping his thumb in and out of her ass. He loved hearing the moans spilling from her mouth but wanted more from her. He released her clit and pulled his thumb away. Hannah whimpered her disapproval.

"What are you doing?" She started to straighten, but before she could sit up, Drew pushed her back down and slapped her ass hard.

"Did I tell you to get up?"

"No, Sir." Her reply was instant.

"Where do you keep your vibrator?" Drew waited only five seconds before slapping her ass again. "Don't feign silence or pretend you don't have one. Tell me."

"In a shoe box in the bottom drawer of my dresser," came the timid reply from the front of the bed.

"That's better. Don't move." Drew rubbed her red ass affectionately before walking over to the dresser and opening the bottom drawer. He found the shoe box under a scarf and pulled it out, opening the cover. He raised an eyebrow in surprise.

"Three, Hannah?" He chuckled as she bobbed her head in silence. She really was made for him. He took the smallest one out before placing the box on top of the dresser and walking back to Hannah.

"You really are a naughty little minx, aren't you?" He kneeled down in front of her head and pulled her face in for a passionate kiss. Their tongues met amid a tangle of mixed groans from them both. He broke away from her, leaving her breathless, then stood up. He trailed his fingers over the length of her body as he strolled back to her bottom.

He laid the vibrator on the bed next to her knee and caressed her ass before running his fingers up the insides of her thighs to her pussy. She was so wet that his fingers easily slipped inside. He gathered her juices and slid his fingers up to her ass again, mixing it with the remains of his cum, circling around her hole.

"Have you ever used one of these in your ass, Hannah?" He picked up the small vibrator and ran it around her wet asshole.

"No, Sir." Her hair swished as she shook her head back and forth, an excited edge to her voice. He groaned inwardly at her willingness and his cock jerked in eagerness. He turned the base of the vibrator, and it whirred to life with a quiet hum. He touched it to her ass. He didn't push, just laid it there while he bent down and sucked her pussy into his mouth. Her whole body arched into him and she moaned, low and guttural.

He released her pussy. "Are you okay?"

"Yes! Oh my god, yes! Don't stop."

He chuckled lightly. "Always so eager, my little kitten."

He obeyed her command though and ran his tongue down the length of her pussy before suckling gently on her clit. He continued to rub the vibrator gently against her hole until she pressed back into it. Grinning through his work, he complied with her silent request, slowly pushing it inside her. He remembered the bliss at taking her ass for the first time at the club and although this wasn't his cock, her complete trust in him filled him with an overwhelming sense of possession.

She arched low, pushing her ass up. She was ready. He released her clit and stood up behind her. He moved his free hand down to her pussy and continued to stroke it as he pushed the vibrator deeper into her ass.

"Ohhh that feels so good. I'm—I'm going to—"

Drew took his hand away from her pussy and smacked her ass hard three times, pushing the vibrator in all the way at the same time. He wasn't sure if she was yelling in pain or pleasure, but he wasn't about to stop.

"Not yet, Hannah. Wait." Sweat coated his body and his cock was throbbing as he gripped it to line himself up with her core. In one swift motion, he thrust his cock deep inside her pussy.

Hannah groaned and pushed herself up off her shoulders as he drove himself deeper. Drew yanked both of her arms behind her back, grasping her by the elbows, and began thrusting. With each thrust of his cock, he hit the vibrator, ramming it deeper inside her. Hannah's chest was driven forward, her head thrown back, hair falling loose onto her back, mewling sounds leaving her rounded lips. Drew's cock swelled larger with each thrust, and he gripped Hannah tighter, bringing her head close to his lips.

He whispered in her ear, "Come, Hannah. Come now."

As soon as he said the words, her body tightened and convulsed around his cock, a cry rolling off her lips. He wrapped his arms around her middle, jerking her against him as he thrust one more time, his release bursting into her as he sank his teeth into her shoulder, muffling the groan coming from his own throat. He held her tighter as her body spasmed in response to him, then ran his tongue over the mark he had left on her.

Without disconnecting from her, he reached between them and eased the vibrator from her. Upon its release, her pussy squeezed and pulsed around his cock. She melted into him and whimpered as another small release took her. He clicked the vibrator off, dropped it on the floor and then lowered them to the bed. As he spooned her, her heart beat against his chest like a bird taking flight. He pressed small kisses up her neck and across her cheek until he found her lips.

She turned her head and pressed her lips hard against his, thrusting her tongue into his mouth. He darted his tongue out to meet hers and licked her softly, gently, trying to cool her down and bring her back to earth. "What have you done to me? I want more of you. I can't get enough of you."

Her kisses more frantic, she began nipping at his lower lip. She tried to turn and face him, but he gripped her tight. "Let me go!"

"Hannah, shhh." Drew loosened his grip a little, but not entirely, and started stroking one hand lightly up and down her body. "You need to let your mind catch up to your body."

"My body wants more. Who cares what my mind says!" She wriggled in his arms, trying to break free. This time he let her loose. She turned toward him.

"How can I still want you? After what you just did to me?" She looked at him, wide-eyed. "I've never felt like this before."

Drew chuckled as she straddled him, her fingers roaming over his chest.

"Are you laughing at me?" She was starting to look a bit wild now.

He shook his head and then stroked his hands up and down her arms before hauling her down and against him. "No, not at you. Just the situation."

She pulled herself back up into a sitting position, a look of despair on her face. "What situation? Me wanting more of you?"

"This is actually a pretty common occurrence for a submissive."

"A submissive?"

Drew pushed up to a sitting position, leaving Hannah straddled on his lap, but now looking her in the eye. "Well, yes. You gave yourself over completely to me. It's not unusual after that happens the first time to want to give even more of yourself. Your only longing is to please your Master."

"My 'Master'?" She spat it out like a dirty word.

Drew rolled his eyes in dismissal. "Obviously, I'm not your Master. But you did allow me to be your Dominant. And you gave me complete power over you. Whether or not you realize what you did, you surrendered yourself completely. And your endorphins loved it. Your body loved it. It's what drives most submissives."

"But this wasn't the first time I was submissive to you."

Drew's head fell back as he laughed. "Are you kidding me? When we were at Baton, getting you to submit to me was a challenge. You did only what you had to. Tonight, you gave yourself to me because you wanted to."

Hannah was silent for a moment, staring into Drew's eyes. "You're right."

"I know."

Hannah shook her head in feigned annoyance, a small smile forming on her lips. "I hate when you're right."

"I usually am. Get used to it."

Hannah ran her fingers up Drew's chest and neck before wrapping them around his head and weaving them into his hair. She leaned forward and ran the tip of her tongue along his lower lip before biting down gently on it.

Drew pulled her flush against him, moving his mouth against hers in a kiss. One hand latched onto the back of her neck, while the other one trailed down her back, pulling her closer. She rocked her pelvis into his, releasing her grip on his hair, clutching his biceps for leverage.

Drew broke the kiss and pushed her back a bit, a smile on his face. "I guess you don't know how to take no for an answer?"

Hannah continued rocking her core against his pelvis, a pout forming on her lips. "This is your fault. You've created a monster."

"Ha! My fault? I say it's your fault. If you weren't so fucking perfect, I wouldn't have gone crazy trying to find you again."

She surged forward, crashing her lips to his in a bruising kiss, their mouths melting together once again. When she pulled away, she kept her forehead against his. "I'm so glad you saw me in the hotel that day. I'm so glad you didn't leave me alone."

Drew brought his lips to hers again and kissed her quickly. "Me too, Hannah. But I'm still not having sex with you again."

Her eyebrows shot up as he lifted her off him in one smooth motion before sitting her back down beside him. "At least, not for another half hour." And then he waggled his eyebrows at her as he grinned.

H annah rolled over and hit the snooze button on her alarm clock on the bedside table without lifting her head off her pillow. *Why am I so goddamn tired?*

And then, as the fogginess of sleep left her head, a smile broke across her face as she remembered her night with Drew. *Shit, Drew!*

She sat straight up in bed and looked next to her but found

only rumpled bed covers where he had been the night before. She brought her hand to her mouth, trying to cover the smile that refused to disappear, and giggled. She was like a little school girl with a mad crush. It had been a long time since she had let herself feel this happy. It felt almost criminal.

She stretched her arms over her head, feeling every muscle and every wonderful ache from the amazing sex. Yum. She wanted more of this feeling and stat. As she swung her feet out of bed, she reached for the folded piece of paper with her name on it next to the alarm clock.

Good morning beautiful,

I'm sorry I stole away like a thief in the night, but I didn't want to confuse Grace. Dinner Thursday? I have a meeting tonight I can't change. Call or text me.

xx Drew

P.S. You're even more gorgeous when you're sleeping.

Hannah pressed the note to her chest, still smiling. Good lord, I need to get a grip on myself! Her door burst open and Grace ran in, climbed up on her bed and started jumping up and down.

"Mommy, Mommy, Mommy! I'm hungry, Mommy!"

She picked Grace up off the bed. "Good morning, monkey bean. No jumping on the bed."

"But Mommy, monkeys love jumping on beds!"

"Yeah, yeah. Okay, let's go get ready for our day. Come on." Hannah shepherded Grace out of the room and into the kitchen to start their day. One hour later, she had dropped Grace off at Miss Daisy's and was back at the shop, unlocking the door. She was humming through the store, a silly smile still plastered on her face, when her phone dinged. Digging through her bag, she found her phone and checked the screen.

What do you send a girl to thank her for an amazing night if she owns a flower shop?

A smile broke across Hannah's face. She hit reply and typed in a quick response.

I could think of a few things . . .

It took less than a minute for a new reply to appear.

You really are a naughty little minx. I'm missing you this morning. Can you do dinner Thursday night?

Hannah thought for a moment before responding.

I'll have to see if I can get a sitter. I'll let you know later today. I miss you more.

Another message popped up on her window.

I'll be waiting.

Hannah clutched the phone to her chest. Was she taking things too quickly? Before she could overthink it, she texted Tammy to ask if she could take Grace on Thursday night. It wasn't unusual for them to take each other's kid for the night every now and then, but it was rare that they did it during the week. Of course, predictably, her phone rang three minutes later.

"Hello, Tammy."

"Hannah Banana. Why do you need me to take Gracie on a Thursday night? Does it have anything to do with Mr. Tie Me Up and Take Me Home from the hospital?"

Hannah laughed. "Jeez, Tammy. Mr. Tie Me Up? Really?"

"Well, he's the one. Right? From that weekend?"

Hannah sighed, silently wishing she had held back some of the information about the weekend she had spent with Drew.

"Yes, he's the one."

"Oh. My. God. I knew it. Hannah, he's fricking gorgeous. What the hell were you thinking trying to stay away from him?"

"You know what I was trying to do."

"Well, what are you doing now then? Make up your mind girl!"

Hannah groaned, hating that she had to explain herself to her sister. "I know, I know. Believe me, I was trying to keep my life separate from all that, and from him. But he doesn't care. He likes Grace. I talked to him. He made me feel better. Safer about things. So, I don't know."

"Good for you. It's about time you found some happiness again."

"Well, so far he makes me happy. We'll see what happens. I mean, he's a freaking gazillionaire. What do I do with that?"

"Whatever he'll let you!" They both laughed then.

"Seriously, Hannah. This is a good thing. Just go with it. And of course I'll take Gracie on Thursday. I'll pick her up from Miss Daisy's, so just send her with a bag tomorrow, okay?"

"Thanks, Tam. You're the best, really."

CHAPTER EIGHT

H is phone dinged and he picked it up, scanning the screen, a smile stretching across his face.

"Felicia?"

She popped her head in his office doorway a second later. "Yes, sir?"

"Could you make a reservation at Marea for seven-thirty tomorrow evening?"

"Of course. For how many?"

"Two please. Tell them it's for me and ask if I can have a booth by the window."

"Consider it done. Anything else?"

"That's it. Thank you." Her head disappeared from his doorway. "Actually, one more thing, Felicia."

This time her whole body framed the doorway. "Yes?"

"Can you ask the maître d' to arrange a round vase of white roses on the table?"

Felicia looked down, trying to hide the smile breaking out across her face. "Of course."

He waved her away. "Okay, I'm done."

She turned and disappeared from view again. Drew shook his

head. He was turning into a regular sap. But damn it, he would do anything he could to make Hannah feel special.

He hadn't expected to meet anyone who made him feel this way again. After the betrayal of his first wife, he'd closed his heart and satisfied his physical needs at Baton Timide. That had been a fine arrangement up until a few months ago. Something had changed for him the moment he'd seen Hannah and then when he'd heard her voice. He hadn't believed in love at first sight, but now, maybe.

Love was something he hadn't thought he'd ever find again, and now that he possibly had, he was going to do everything right. His first wife had felt slighted by the demands of his job. He didn't want to make that mistake again with Hannah. He needed to make sure she realized she was special to him, especially because Hannah's heart wasn't the only one at stake here. She had a beautiful little girl who was obviously her whole world. Another thing he had never factored into his life. He shook his head in an attempt to clear his thoughts. As usual, he was trying to force all the pieces into place before they were even laid out. Him and his damn control issues.

He pushed back from his desk, grabbed his jacket out of the closet and left his office. "Felicia, I'll be out for a few hours. I have my cell if you need me."

"Yes, sir."

Drew took the elevator down to the lobby, strolled out of the hotel exit, then headed toward Fifth Avenue. He was going to make sure Hannah knew how special she was to him. How special she was period. He walked into Saks with a smile on his face.

"Hannah, there's a delivery for you," Robin called from the front of the store.

Hannah stood and walked out to the main showroom to find

three black boxes wrapped in a red satin ribbon on the counter. "What's this?" She looked at Robin curiously.

Robin shrugged, then grinned and handed Hannah an envelope. "Not sure, but a delivery guy just dropped it off and said it was for you. And it's from Saks!"

Hannah regarded the packages warily and took the envelope from Robin. She ran her finger under the closure to open and pull the note card out. The initials AMS were embossed on the front of the card in dark sapphire ink. Drew. She brought the card up to her nose and inhaled. She closed her eyes as she picked up the lingering scent of him on the paper. Opening her eyes, and then the card, she read the short note:

Hannah,

I'd be so pleased if you would wear this to dinner this evening.

And just this. XX Drew

This felt unsettlingly familiar. She thought her days of being told how to dress were over. She placed the card down on the counter and pulled the ribbon from the boxes. What was inside? She quickly slid the cover off the smallest box and pulled the tissue paper aside. She blushed at the black lace garter and nude silk stockings, knowing Robin was watching.

"Sexy!" Robin squealed and tried to reach inside to touch them, but Hannah quickly folded the tissue paper back into place.

Yes, definitely starting to feel like a submissive at Baton Timide again.

"Too personal," Hannah chided.

"Let's see what's in the next box!" Robin prompted, undeterred.

Hannah pulled the cover off the second box. Her heart screeched to a halt. A tan Christian Louboutin Paris shoe box. These types of purchases were so out of her league. She bought her shoes off the sale rack at Macy's, and they never ever had a red sole on them.

Her mouth open in shock, she turned toward Robin. "Are you seeing what I'm seeing?"

"Holy hell. Open that damn box already, woman."

With trembling hands, Hannah pulled the Louboutin box out

of the larger box and set it on the counter before yanking the cover off. Inside was a red felt bag, which she took and set on the counter. Loosening the draw string, she reached in and slid out a pair of four-inch black satin pumps with delicate ankle straps. She placed them on the counter and ran her fingers over the material.

"These are too much. I could never wear something like these."

"If you don't, I'll figure out a way to squeeze my size eight feet into them. They're gorgeous." Robin picked one up and turned it upside down, exposing the red sole.

"Do you know how expensive shoes like this are?" Hannah snagged the shoe from Robin. "Seriously, these would probably pay half my monthly mortgage on this place. This feels so wrong to me. I don't need something like this."

Robin's fisted hands fell to her hips, a frown appearing on her face. "Why shouldn't you be spoiled like this? It's about time someone realized how special you are and scooped you up."

Despite her queasy stomach, Hannah smiled warmly at her friend. "No more special than you."

"Are you going to open the last box or what?" Robin pressed.

Hannah's hands wrung together as she viewed the rest of the packages. "God, I don't know. This is already too much. I feel like I should just wrap everything back up and return it."

"Don't be ridiculous. He wanted you to have these things. And let's face it, it has to be something to go with those shoes. Maybe it's a trench coat and he wants you to show up in just that, the heels and undies."

Hannah slapped her friend lightly on the shoulder. "Oh my god, don't even go there!"

"I know, right?" Robin let out an excited giggle. "This is totally bananas! This only happens in the movies!"

Hannah slid the cover off of the third box and started to pull back the tissue paper but stopped abruptly at the sight of a blue tiffany box. Her breath caught in her throat even as her heart started galloping in her chest. Not another blue box. Hadn't he heard her when she'd said they needed to take things slow? Having sex was one thing, but there was no way he was putting any type of collar on her. This was not Baton Timide. She was not his submissive anymore. She wanted to be his girlfriend, his equal. Well, okay, he could boss her around in the bedroom and she wouldn't complain about that.

"Oh my. Tiffany's too?" Robin cooed enviously.

Hannah just shook her head in disappointment. Instead of opening the Tiffany box, she just took it out and placed it to the side.

"Wait, you're not going to open it?"

She shook her head and murmured, "Not right now. Maybe later." She pulled back the rest of the tissue paper to reveal a black wrap-style dress.

"That's an Alexandre Vauthier dress." While Robin's voice was filled with envy as she pointed at the label, Hannah's insides were twisting into knots. She didn't want to be dressed like a doll. She wanted Drew to trust her enough to dress herself. She felt like she was being bought all over again.

She picked the dress up and shook it out so she could see it in its entirety. The material was gorgeous. It had a soft, rayon feel to it, but with more structure. It looked like an oversized suit jacket with a deep V in the front, but without the lapels. The dress wrapped around at the waist and was held together with a wide belt in the same material.

"It looks like a coat. That's going to be mighty short on those long legs, Hannah."

"I was just thinking the same thing." Not really, but she would at least let Robin enjoy the moment. She folded the dress and placed it back in the box, replacing the cover.

"Are you sure you don't want to open up that blue box?" Robin urged, a look of desire on her face.

Hannah shook her head again. "Positive."

"Ya know, it's already two o'clock. I can handle the store if you want to head upstairs early and start your beauty prep now."

"I wouldn't mind leaving early if you think you can handle the shop?"

"Go. But promise me that you'll tell me all the details tomorrow!"

"Of course!" Hannah gave Robin a hug, wondering as she did, what in the hell she was going to do with these "gifts."

Hannah went into the back room and put her jacket on before grabbing all the boxes and heading up to her apartment. As soon as she put the boxes down, she dug her phone out of her purse to text Drew.

Thank you for the lovely gifts, but it's too much. I insist you take them back.

Several moments ticked by as she waited for him to respond. Staring at her phone wasn't helping, so she went to the fridge and pulled out a bottle of water. As soon as she turned the cap to open it, her phone dinged.

You're welcome. And I insist you keep them. It makes me happy to buy gifts for you. Besides, I can't wait to see you in that dress.

Hannah slammed the water bottle down and began typing.

I'm not a sub at Baton that you can dress at will. Please take them back. Especially that damn blue box.

More than several minutes passed. Her mind was racing at what his reply would be. Finally, a half bottle of water later—and a half mile of pacing—her phone dinged.

I wasn't dressing you like a sub. I simply wanted to make you feel special. Wear whatever makes you comfortable. My apologies.

She felt a pang of regret. Had she overreacted? Was she being too sensitive? She'd never dated a man with money before and wasn't used to receiving gifts of any sort.

Sorry. This is still all new to me. And the blue box may have pushed me over the edge.

His reply came only a second later.

Apology accepted. It's not a collar. Bring it with you

tonight. I'll see if I can change your mind. Pick you up at 7?
She frowned in wonder as she replied.
See you at 7.

D rew stepped out of the town car and adjusted his jacket. He was wearing a dark slate suit, a crisp white shirt and a gray and black print tie. He pulled on his overcoat and walked into the alley beside the flower shop. It was exactly one minute until seven; he was nothing if not prompt. He rang the apartment doorbell and waited, pacing back and forth.

A few moments later the door swung open and he spun around to a stunning Hannah. She stood in the doorway, still as a post, clutching her coat and purse with white knuckles, her lower lip caught between her lip. She was wearing the outfit he'd sent. He raked his gaze over her, starting at her softly curled hair and ruby red lips, down to the swell of her breasts exposed in the deep V of the dress, farther down to her silk-covered legs and, finally, to feet clad in the sexiest pair of pumps, strapped tightly to her ankles.

He let out a slow whistle. "Good evening, Hannah."

"Drew." She cast her head downward as a small smile danced across her lips.

He put a finger under her chin and lifted it a fraction so that he could look into her eyes. "You may be the sexiest thing I have ever seen."

Her cheeks turned a light shade of pink. "Thank you. You are looking pretty fine yourself, Mr. Sapphire."

He bent and brushed his lips against her painted ones. "Thank you for wearing the dress. It suits you. But, just to be clear, you would look amazing in anything."

He watched as she swept her hand down the short length of the dress, trying to pull it down lower when she reached the hem. "There's not very much of it."

A mischievous grin lit up his face as he pulled her hand away from the hem. With a single finger, he pushed the hem up her thigh an inch, stopping at the strap of the garter belt attached to the top of her stalking. He slid his finger to the inside of her thigh before slipping it farther north. When he bumped against her bare core, she inhaled sharply and stopped his hand with hers.

He tilted his head before whispering in her ear. "You just got me so goddamn hard."

He trailed his finger back down her thigh as he leaned in further, languorously kissed her neck . She tipped her head to the side and let out a small stuttered sigh. He pulled his lips away from her neck and stepped back, taking her coat from her hand at the same time. Her eyes locked with his in desire as he held the coat open for her. She turned, gracefully stepping into the coat. He gently spun her around, holding her eyes again as he buttoned her jacket up.

"Ready?"

"We could just stay here." Her response was breathy and filled with longing.

He chuckled and shook his head. "Nope. I'm taking you on a date." He placed his hand on the small of her back and guided her to the waiting car.

"We could just have our date here." She looked coyly over her shoulder at him.

"Oh, you are always so anxious, my little kitten. I've got plans for you tonight."

They reached the town car, and the driver opened the back door.

"You're not driving?" she asked.

"Not tonight." He turned and held her hand as she sat down in the car. "I wanted to keep my hands free."

Her eyes widened at his statement and a smile curved her lips, her eyes darting to the driver. Drew waited until she was seated comfortably, then moved to the other side of the car and climbed in beside her. "Come closer."

She scooted across the seat until she was up against his thigh.

He pulled the bottom of her jacket open and rested his hand on the inside of her thigh. He leaned in and inhaled deeply.

"You always smell so good, Hannah. Like springtime."

"Really? I'm not wearing perfume." She brought the back of her hand up to her nose and sniffed.

"I know you aren't. It's just you. It's one of the things I love about you."

She looked over at him quickly and then back down at her hands. "So where are we going?"

He moved his thumb in small circles on the inside of her thigh, loving the soft feeling of the silk. "A restaurant called Marea. Do you know it?"

"I've heard of it. I've never been of course."

He trailed his fingers higher until he reached bare thigh, moving his thumb in small circles. He bent closer. "Open your legs wider."

Her eyes shot to the driver and then back to him.

"Don't worry about him. David's worked for me for years."

Hannah scooted up higher in the seat and snapped her legs shut in the same motion. Drew shook his head, then used his trapped hand to pinch her inner thigh. She squeaked in surprise, and her legs popped open again.

He leaned down and whispered in her ear, brushing his lips against her skin as he did. "Don't fight me." He ran his tongue around the rim of her ear, then down the side of her neck.

He grinned at the low whimper that escaped her, and her legs widened further. Her breath hitched when his finger brushed against her clit, and then his own hitched when he felt how wet she was. He moved his lips back up to her ear.

"You're already so fucking wet."

She turned her head so that her lips were against his and started kissing him hungrily. He slid his free hand around the nape of her neck, pulling her in tighter, pushing his tongue against her lips in demand. She complied immediately, their tongues dancing as their kiss deepened. He slid his finger back and forth against the hard hood of her clit, teasing a deep growl from the back of Hannah's throat.

He pulled his mouth away from hers and brought it back to her ear. "You like that?"

She nodded, pushing her core harder against his fingers. He chuckled low and deep at her neediness before thrusting not one, but two fingers into her. Her hand gripped his arm tightly, her teeth clamping onto her lower lip as her eyes opened wide in surprise.

"Drew, please!" She was practically panting as she whispered.

He looked at her, a feral gleam in his eye. He fucking loved seeing her wither for him. His cock was so goddamn hard in his trousers. "Please what?"

"Make me come or stop," she breathed, continuing to clutch his arm, her face pinking at her bold request.

The car suddenly stopped and a voice came from the front. "We're here, Mr. Sapphire."

"Very good. Just give us a moment please."

"Of course." David left the car running but opened the door and stepped out, standing beside the now closed door.

Drew turned his attention back to Hannah, his fingers still working in and out of her pussy. "I'm going to make you come so many times tonight, you'll be begging me to stop."

And then he hooked his fingers, driving them deeper into her, pushing hard against her clit at the same time. "Come, but don't make a sound."

Her muscles clenched tightly around his fingers and then pulsed, her grip on his arm tightening even more, her teeth biting down on her bottom lip as breath whooshed from her nose. He rocked his fingers slowly now, riding out her orgasm until she started to relax and her grip on him loosened.

He bent down and bit her bottom lip, pulling it from her teeth, and then kissed her hard, stealing her breath from her.

"That's number one. Let's keep count, shall we?"

Her eyes closed tightly and she exhaled heavily before she

spoke. "You're going to kill me."

He slid his fingers out of her slowly, watching her lips form a small O when he pulled free from her. His throbbing cock twitched. He brought his fingers to his mouth, sealing his lips around them, closing his eyes as he sucked, savoring the taste of her. He slowly drew them out, his gaze finding Hannah's wide one. "So unbelievably fucking good. I could skip dinner and just eat you."

"Okay." She didn't even miss a beat.

He shook his head in disbelief at her eagerness. "As appealing as that sounds, it will have to wait. I need to feed you if you're going to have enough energy tonight."

Hannah's eyes lit up. She was so responsive to his every wish or command. "Okay."

He covered his cock with her hand. Her eyes flew up to his. "Do you see what you do to me? So fucking hard, Hannah."

She started stroking up and down his shaft but he dropped his hand over hers, stilling her motion. "No. I'll explode in two minutes if you do that."

She mewled desperately. "Let me make you feel good."

He shook his head. "No, I can wait."

She stuck her lower lip out in a pout and shrugged her shoulders. "If you're sure."

"I am." He leaned over and kissed her lips roughly and then broke away from her again. "I'm going to step outside for a moment and cool down. Take a moment if you need it."

She used her fingers to wipe away her lipstick from his mouth. He smiled at her attention and then pulled his overcoat closed as he opened the back door to step outside.

Hannah shook her head at what she had allowed Drew to do to her in the car—while someone else had been two feet away! She blew out a breath and then reached into her purse to find her powder and lipstick. She quickly reapplied both and then did her best to pull the very short dress down and back into place.

The sight of the garter straps, visible when she was sitting, made her turn crimson. She had never worn anything this provocative. While it felt so terribly indecent, she couldn't help feeling incredibly sexy at the same time. And the way Drew had looked at her in it, had made her core instantly tighten. This man made her feel things and want to do things she had never imagined. And the worst of it was, she wanted more.

Shaking her head at herself, she pulled her jacket close around her and pushed her door open. Drew was there, waiting, and before she could even step out of the car, his hand was there to guide her up. When she was fully out, he pulled her to his side and kissed the side of her temple. "All set?"

"Yes. I'm good."

"Okay, right this way then."

He kept his hand on the small of her back as he led her into the restaurant. Inside, light piano music tinkled from somewhere, and lit candles decorated every table. The restaurant was decked out in beautiful reds and whites, romantic lighting and a gorgeous fire burning along a back wall. He checked their coats and then approached the hostess.

She followed as the hostess led them to a table in the back of the room, close to the fireplace. Hannah felt like every set of eyes in the restaurant was watching her as she walked to their booth. Like they knew she was playing dress-up and was an imposter at their party. Goose bumps broke out across her arms and a shiver ran down her spine.

Drew turned toward her, his face concerned, "You okay?"

She nodded once, smiling. "Just a chill."

"Will this do, Mr. Sapphire?" The hostess swung her hand wide at the table in question. The table, lit by a silver candelabra, held a round vase full of white roses.

"It's perfect."

Drew held out one of the chairs for her. As she sat, the hostess came over and presented her with a menu and then one to Drew, who was now sitting. She smiled and told them to enjoy their evening before leaving. Hannah could still feel eyes looking at her and opened the menu up in an attempt to block them out.

Drew's fingers fell on top of her menu and pushed it down. "Hey, you okay?"

She shook her head back and forth and glanced around the room before whispering, "Everyone's looking at me."

Drew glanced around the room and then back at her. "You're a beautiful woman. It's normal for people to admire a beautiful woman when they see her."

"I feel like everyone here knows I don't belong."

His brow furrowed deeply. "Why would you ever feel that way?"

"I grew up in rural New York and I work at a flower shop. The fanciest thing I've ever done is go to the masquerade ball you brought me to."

He pulled the menu completely from her hands, placed it on the table and then took her hands in his. "When you walk, when you talk, the way you treat people; it is nothing short of graceful. That's not something that comes with money."

She extricated her hands from his and sat up straight in her chair. He was trying so hard and she was ruining things. "I'm sorry, Drew. The restaurant really is lovely."

He smiled back at her but it was strained. "Thank you for coming with me. I don't think I've ever had a more beautiful date."

Her features softened. "Nor I. Thank you."

"I'd give you the moon and the stars if you'd let me," he murmured before turning his attention toward the wine menu, as if the admission embarrassed him. She flushed at his confession and reached for her own menu.

The waitress came over and took their order for a bottle of red wine. She was back in moments, popping the cork and pouring Drew a sample to taste. Upon his approval, she filled each of their glasses and took their order for dinner. Well, Drew's order for their dinners. He had ordered them both a four-course dinner consisting of antipasto, mushroom risotto, thyme-crusted lamb with baby fingerling potatoes and chocolate soufflés for dessert.

She leaned forward and hissed through clenched teeth, "What if I had wanted something different?"

A look of surprise crossed his face. "I'm sorry. I should have asked. I'm used to just ordering. It was presumptuous of me. Would you like something different?"

Hannah looked around before answering to make sure no one would overhear her. "No, it's fine, but I can't eat all of that. The risotto would have been plenty and this place is very expensive. It will be wasted."

A wide smile broke across Drew's face. "You know I'm a billionaire, right?"

She did not smile back. "So? Does that mean you should waste your money? And once again, you're treating me like a submissive." She lowered her voice to a whisper edged in anger. "Are you going to feed me my food too?"

Drew's lips pursed into a tight line. "First, I love that you're worried about spending my money. That's a new one for me. But believe me, I'm fine." His tone was clearly edged with sarcasm. "And as far as the way I'm treating you, I'm simply trying to be a gentleman. It's not uncommon or considered in bad taste to order for your date."

Hannah looked down in embarrassment. She kept jumping to conclusions about the way he was treating her and it was ruining the evening. "I'm sorry. You're trying so hard to treat me like a lady and I'm just treating you awfully. I'm so out of my depth."

Drew took her hand from across the table. "Hannah, being with you . . . the feelings you stir in me . . . I'm the one that's out of my depth."

She stared in shock at his admission. "Really? I'm speechless."

Drew huffed, a wide smile breaking across his face. "Finally!"

She rolled her eyes, relieved the tense moment was broken, and let out a nervous laugh. A moment later their first course arrived and they started to eat. The antipasto was amazing. The strained silence was not.

"Do you normally eat out every night?" She needed to know more about his everyday life if she was ever going to understand him, and frankly, the silence was deafening.

He shook his head. "No, not usually. Unless I have a business meeting. David—my driver from the car?"

"Yes?"

"He is also my head of security and personal protection detail when required. He and his wife Julie have a suite of their own at the hotel. Julie cooks and cleans for me when I stay at the hotel. Takes care of my dry cleaning, makes sure my fridge is stocked."

"Wait, all I got out of that is *personal protection detail*. What does that mean?"

Drew shrugged. "I'm rich. Sometimes I need someone to have my back."

"You mean, like a bodyguard?" She set her fork down on her plate.

Again, he shrugged. "Eh, call it what you will."

She scoffed. "I call it a bodyguard." She frowned, her brow crinkling. "But I've never seen David or anyone else with you before."

"I don't need one in most circumstances. There are occasions when I do though, and then I have David."

Her eyes widened a bit. "So, is he your driver or your bodyguard tonight?"

He shook his head and chuckled. "My driver."

"The rich are very complicated people." She took another bite of her food.

"Not just the rich." He tilted his head, sarcasm dripping from his tone.

Her brow furrowed at his slight dig, but before she could respond, a server interrupted them to clear their salad plates and set the risotto down in front of them.

"Okay, I'm changing the subject. Where does your family live? Ben and your mother and father? Do they live at the hotel too?"

"Twenty questions tonight?" He had a tired smile on his face.

Her voice grew quiet. "I just want to know you better."

He stared at her a moment while he took a sip of his wine. "Okay, I have a question for you then."

She nodded. "Okay."

"Did you bring the Tiffany box with you?"

She sat up straighter. "Oh, not what I was expecting."

He raised his eyebrows. "What were you expecting?"

"Not sure." She reached down to the floor and brought her purse up to the table. "But yes, I brought it." She opened her purse and pulled the box out, placing it on the table between them.

"Open it." His eyes locked onto hers.

"No." She reached for her wine glass and took a sip.

"Open it, Hannah." Commanding this time. His eyes remaining locked in place.

She hesitated a moment and then muttered, "I don't want to. I'm afraid of what's in there."

"I already told you it's not a collar." His reply was gentle this time.

"I know. But it's a Tiffany box."

He tilted his head in confusion. "And?"

"So out of my depth again, Drew."

He pulled her fingers into his. "Stop saying that. And just open the damn box." He released her and slid the box directly in front of her.

She looked up at him warily and then, with shaking fingers, lifted the lid off the box. Her eyes flew up to his, her cheeks lifting in a smile. "It's lovely."

She lowered her gaze back to the contents, her fingers grazing lightly over a silver chain necklace that ended with a tassel made of small pearls, held together by a delicately decorated silver cap. Also inside were matching pearl drop earrings.

"See, nothing bad." His lips lifting slightly.

She looked away from the box to meet his eyes. "But why? Why do you keep doing these things? It's too much."

He moved his finger lightly over the cap holding the pearl tassel together. "Do you see this?"

Hannah nodded.

"This design is made up of olive leaves. And I'm thankful—" He stopped and looked up at her then, removing the necklace from the box before standing up. Stepping behind her, he brushed her hair over one shoulder and then draped the necklace around her neck, fastening it.

"I'm so grateful you gave me a second chance. Extending the olive branch, so to speak." His fingers trailed down the length of the necklace, which fell between the curve of her breasts, and then back up, before moving her hair back into place. He bent down, kissed her cheek and returned to his chair.

Hannah looked down. The necklace sat perfectly in the low V of the dress. Everything Drew did had a purpose. A pang of guilt shot through her for her belligerent behavior toward him all evening. She ran her fingers down the silver chain, stopping when she reached the silver tassels.

"Thank you, Drew. You keep doing things for me out of the kindness of your heart, and I keep accusing you of bad behavior. I'm not sure I deserve your gratitude."

He nodded at her admission. "We'll figure it out. Both of us."

She sighed. "You're probably too good for me."

He rolled his eyes and let out a small, dark laugh. "I could punish you. And before you say anything, yes, now I am taking control."

"That kind of control I like." Her voice grew hoarse.

"You definitely are going to keep me on my toes."

"Can we go please?"

"Are you not hungry?"

Her eyes met his, her reply raspy. "For you."

Drew raised his hand and motioned for the waitress. "Check please."

CHAPTER NINE

With a hand at the small of her back, Drew steered Hannah through the lobby of the hotel and to the elevator. Stepping inside, he keyed in the security code to his suite. Then, without warning, he turned and shoved Hannah up against the wall. She gasped in surprise but melted into him.

"Always my eager little kitten." He bent down and nibbled on her neck as he worked the buttons of her coat open. He reached inside and splayed his hands around her center, pushing her harder against the elevator wall. He grinned wickedly and then trailed his tongue down the base of her neck to the bottom of the V in her dress.

Hannah's head rolled to the side and a breathy sigh escaped her parted lips until Drew leaned back up and slammed his mouth over hers. He hissed as her hands wrapped around his neck, pulling at the hair at his nape.

The elevator dinged and the doors slid open to deliver them to the entryway of his suite. Not breaking their lip-lock, he turned her at the waist and guided her into the suite, pinning her back up against the wall in the hallway.

As he continued stroking her lips with his own, he ground his pelvis into hers, showing her how hard she made him. She pushed him away and started shaking her coat off.

"Too hot" was all she said before dropping the coat on the floor, watching as he also shed his. He chuckled as she reached for his shirt to pull him closer. She loosened his tie and tugged it over his head, then started working on the buttons of his shirt.

"Let me help." He pushed her hands away and, with a smirk, took both sides of his shirt and yanked it apart, buttons popping off. He slid it off his shoulders. Her eyes flew open and she licked her lips before dropping both hands to his bare chest and running them lower to his belt.

"Stop."

Her hands stilled and her eyes peeked up at him in question. He raised her hands above her head, pushing them against the wall.

"Leave them like that."

She blinked slowly and looked down submissively. "Yes, Sir."

His cock jutted in his pants at her obedience and he rewarded her with a searing kiss. "Good girl."

He slid his fingers under the wide belt holding her dress together and unclasped the hooks. The belt fell loose as he spread the dress apart, exposing her breasts and bare center. He placed both of his hands on her taut stomach and trailed them slowly up until they were each cupping a breast. He massaged them gently before taking one hard pebble in his mouth, biting down gently.

Hannah's back arched off the wall as she cried out. He shoved her back flat against the wall, not releasing the nipple, instead sucking it harder into his mouth. Mewling sounds left her lips each time he alternated between biting and sucking, and he had to keep his hand pressed firmly against her center to keep her from rocking into him. He finally released her nipple, laving his tongue over it and then up her neck until his lips found hers again.

She kissed him desperately, shoving her tongue deep in his mouth, moaning as she did. Drew pulled back and looked her in the eye, her mouth red and swollen.

"What do you want, Hannah?"

She blinked once and whispered, "You."

"I'm yours." He growled. "What do you want?"

She looked at him in silence for a few moments before answering. "I want you in my mouth."

Drew let a moan fall from his lips and leaned his forehead against hers. "You are fucking perfect."

He kissed her then, slowly, tenderly. "Put your hands down."

He stepped back and watched her lower her hands and shake them a bit. "Take your dress off."

She let the dress fall off one shoulder, then pulled the other side off and let the dress fall to the floor. He just stared at her. She wore only the necklace, garters and heels and was the most fucking unbelievable sight to behold. "Walk to the living room and stand by the couch."

He wanted to watch her ass as she walked. The lace of the garter fell halfway down each ass cheek, where it met the strap attached to the stockings. As she walked, her ass exposed and lifted high from the heels, he couldn't help but reach down and shift his cock before it shot out of his pants. She reached the couch and stood, head down, waiting.

He followed, then grabbed one of the cushions off the back of the couch and dropped it flat on the floor in front of her. "Get on your knees."

She dropped immediately to the cushion. "Unbutton my pants and release my cock."

Hannah looked up at him through her lashes and moved her hands to his pants, working his belt and then the button on the trousers before pulling them down. He was commando, so his hard cock jutted free as it was released from its prison.

He sighed in relief when her hand grasped him around his base and slowly sucked his cock into her hot mouth. She hummed around his length, and he had to grab onto the top of her head to steady himself from the fucking pleasure of it. She brought her other hand up, grasping him now with two hands, squeezing tight, while continuing to suck his shaft in and out of her mouth.

He growled at the sensation and knew he would come if he didn't stop her. He tightened his grasp on her head and pulled her back off his cock.

She looked up at him, her eyes wide. "I'm not done."

He snarled, tugging on her hair in an indication she should rise. "Yes you are."

When she was standing straight in front of him, he crashed his lips to hers, yanking her body flush. His cock, wet from her mouth, slid against her belly. The friction was enough to drive him over the edge, so he tore his lips from hers and grasped her by the shoulders, separating them gently. His pants were still around his ankles, so he leaned down and pulled his shoes off, then his pants.

"Go over to the window and stand in front of it."

Hannah looked at him and blew out a breath in frustration. She was getting tired of being made to wait for what she wanted. What she needed.

She took a moment to assess the man standing naked in front of her. He stood tall, lean and muscular, but not bulky. She loved the soft dark curls that started at his chest and sprinkled down into a thin line like an arrow pointing the way to his manhood. She looked longingly at its hardness, licking her lips unconsciously.

"Do it, Hannah. Now."

She turned and stepped lightly to the wall of windows next to the dining room table. She looked at Drew for his next instruction, anxious to get her hands back on his body. He stood watching her from the living room before closing the distance between them, stopping a foot away.

"Turn around, bend over, and place your hands flat on the window."

Her eyebrows raised in question, she looked at the window and then back at him.

"Don't worry, no one can see in. It's one-way glass."

This made her feel a little better. She didn't mind putting on a show for Drew, but not half of Fifty-Ninth Avenue. "Yes, Sir."

She faced the window and bent forward at the waist, placing her hands on the glass as Drew had instructed. When she leaned forward, the necklace around her neck swung forward and the pearls clacked softly against the glass. They continued to swing slowly back and forth in the space between her breasts and the glass as she waited for what came next.

Bending over like this exposed her core to Drew, but instead of feeling embarrassed, she felt empowered and sexy. Knowing she shouldn't, but not being able to resist, she looked over her shoulder at Drew. His fist was around his cock, stroking it languidly, his eyes dark and heavy with lust as they met hers. Not letting go of his length, he took two steps until he was standing directly behind her, shaking his head once.

"Tsk, tsk little kitten. Always so curious." And without warning his free hand smacked her hard across the ass. She sucked in a breath at the contact and opened her stance wider to try and keep her balance. He seized her stinging cheek, rubbing it in small circles with the palm of his hand.

"I think sometimes you want me to punish you. Do you like when I spank you, Hannah?"

She shook her head back and forth in response and was met with another smack on her ass.

"It's 'Yes, Sir' or 'No, Sir.'" His hand fondling her ass again. Her core growing more slick with each touch, whether it be soft or hard.

"No, Sir."

He chuckled and then he slid his hand down her ass and trailed his fingers between her pussy lips, finding her wet and slippery. She couldn't help the soft moan that slipped out of her mouth. "Your pussy tells me a different story, Hannah."

She tried to be still as he worked his fingers back and forth over her clit but she thrust back into him when he plunged two fingers into her. The constant teasing had left her throbbing and his fingers only made her crave more. He crowded forward, dominating her body with his, as he thrust another finger into her and rocked them in and out of her slowly.

Panting, she tilted her hips, trying to push her clit into his fingers, but Drew withdrew before she could trigger a release. She let out a small whine of discontent and whipped her head around. Drew had his fingers in his mouth, sucking, a sly grin on his face. He slid them out, then grasped her by the hips and rubbed his cock up and down the seam of her ass.

"What do you want, Hannah?" His voice was gravelly and thick.

She tried to push back into him, but the grasp he had on her hips made it impossible, frustrating her further. She growled under her breath and was met with another chuckle.

"Just tell me what you want."

Dropping her head in defeat, she sucked in a breath and pleaded, "I want you to fuck me."

"Why didn't you just say so?" In one swift motion, he plunged his cock down into her slick center. Every muscle in her core clenched around him as he seated himself fully. She groaned in satisfaction. He paused like that for a moment, apparently savoring the feeling, then withdrew almost entirely. He surged forward again, driving himself back into her in one hard thrust.

Her entire body surged forward, shoving her face and breasts up against the glass, her necklace clinking. Her peaks grew harder from the cold as she braced her head. Drew's hands encircled her waist, and he pushed down, raising her ass higher as he pulled back out of her slowly again. She knew what to expect this time, and when he thrust again, she welcomed it.

He slid his hands up her waist until he broke the seal between the window and her breasts, cupping each one to pull her back into him and away from the window. She left her hands braced on the glass for support but threw her head back with a loud moan as Drew rolled her hardened peaks between his fingers, thrusting in and out of her at the same time.

He was grunting from the exertion, sweat dripping off of him and onto her back. Each thrust pushed against her throbbing clit, her climax building. As if Drew could sense her impending orgasm, he tugged her back against his body and thrust harder, bringing his lips to her ear, panting.

"I'm going to come, Hannah. Are you ready?"

She swung her head back and forth. "Oh my god, yes! Yes!"

Drew's release exploded like a rush of hot lava, detonating her own climax, her muscles clamping down around his cock before releasing in a thousand pulsing beats. She cried out, her fists clenched, her fingernails scraping across the window. Drew's mouth clamped down on her shoulder, muffling a low roar, his arms tightening around her.

After several moments, Drew's hold on her loosened, his lips brushing kisses across her shoulder as he pulled them both upright. He spun her around in his arms and brought his mouth to hers in a slow, gentle kiss. She wound her arms around his neck, fusing their naked bodies together. His lips left hers and she rolled her head to the side as he dropped kisses down her neck and then back up to her ear.

He ran his tongue across her ear and then blew lightly on it, sending chills over her skin. Her grip tightened, pulling his hair.

"Oh my god, that felt so good."

His grip on her tightened. Then with the softest breath of air, his lips brushed her ear whispering in a low chuckle, "That was only number two."

He picked her up then, wrapping her legs around his waist, and carried her to the bedroom.

Hannah woke early the next morning and blinked until her eyes adjusted to the light. Drew lay next to her still sleeping soundly, his breath drawing in and out of his mouth in a slow rhythm. Her eyes raked down his naked form admiringly, and for about the hundredth time she wondered how she had gotten here, in a gorgeous billionaire's bed. She shook her head in silent disbelief before slipping quietly out from under the covers.

It was already close to seven a.m. and she needed to get home to shower and open the shop. She tiptoed over to the dresser against the wall and, as quietly as possible, pulled open some drawers until she found a sweatshirt and a pair of sweats. They would be huge, but there was no way she was doing the walk of shame across the hotel lobby in the dress from last night.

Shit. She realized she only had her pumps to wear and cursed herself for not getting up and going home last night. Grabbing the shoes in one hand and the stolen clothes in the other, she stepped softly to the door so she could dress in the living room.

"Stay," a low voice grumbled from the bed.

She swung around quickly, a smile breaking across her face. "Sorry. I was trying not to wake you."

"Why are you sneaking out without saying goodbye? Come here." He sat up in the bed and motioned her closer.

She shook her head, her eyes scanning his chiseled torso, the playful smile on his face. "No way, mister. If I come any closer, I know exactly what's going to happen."

"Exactly. So come here."

She started backing away and toward the door again. "Nope. Gotta go home and shower and open the shop. Call me later, okay?"

"I want to see you later. Can I?"

She stilled just for a moment, opened her mouth to speak but then clamped it shut.

He sat up, concern on his face. "What?"

She shook her head. "It's just that I have to work all day, and then I have Grace. We have a bit of a routine. I don't want to confuse her." As much as she wanted to spend time with him, she was also afraid they might be moving too quickly.

He threw the covers off the bed and swung his legs onto the floor. "What if I bring dinner to both of you then? After five? Keep things simple?"

How could she say no to that? "Okay. That sounds good."

He rose up out of the bed and stalked over to her, grabbing her naked body around the waist and pulling her close.

"I'm not letting you leave me until I get at least a good morning kiss." He bent down and pressed his lips to hers in a warm, sultry kiss. She sighed in resignation and kissed him back, loving the taste of him on her lips. Before things could get any more heated, she broke off and pushed him away.

"Only a kiss. I don't have time for more, as much as I'd enjoy it." She grinned shyly, trying hard to keep her eyes away from his hardened length.

"I'll have David take you home. Let me just call him." He walked over to the phone sitting on the table.

She was going to argue, but the thought of everyone in the lobby seeing her in sweats and heels changed her mind. "Okay, if he's available."

He began speaking on the phone and then hung up. "He's available. Take the elevator to P1 and he'll be there waiting."

She smiled gratefully at him and walked over, leaning into him for another kiss. "Thank you."

"Go," he growled through their kiss. "Because if you stay another minute, I'm not letting you leave."

She laughed and pulled away, turning from him to flee from the room.

"Hannah?"

She stopped and looked back over her shoulder.

"I hope last night was okay. I know it was a little awkward in the beginning."

She nodded in agreement. "It was good. Next time, we'll do better."

"Okay, get out. Go to work."

She blew him a kiss over her shoulder and left.

Ten long, busy hours later, Hannah locked the shop door behind her and headed up to her apartment, holding Grace's little hand. The shop was extremely busy prepping and ordering for the upcoming Thanksgiving holiday, and the lack of sleep the night before had kicked in. She was exhausted and all she really wanted to do was crawl into some pajamas and then into bed. She wondered if it was too late to call Drew and cancel. Dinner at her place was going to be nothing like their dinner at the restaurant the night before.

Before she could pick up the phone, the doorbell rang. Sure enough, when she opened the door, there stood Drew. He smiled and held up a large brown paper bag. "I hope Chinese is okay? Maybe eat out of cartons and keep the dishes to a minimum?"

She sighed in relief and motioned for him to come in. "You have no idea how perfect that sounds."

As they made their way into the kitchen, Grace appeared and began chattering away as Drew as unpacked the food. Her worries about a stressful night melted away when she saw how easily the two of them were getting along. Now knowing the relationship he had with his sister, it made so much more sense to her.

After they ate, Drew offered to clean up so Hannah could give Grace a bath and get her settled down for the night. Forty- ive minutes later they were both snuggled on her couch together. She had changed into a pair of yoga pants and a loose T-shirt that hung off her shoulder. Drew's fingers were running in a lazy circle over her exposed skin as they talked about their days.

"By the way, I have to go to Boston for a few days next week. Hotel stuff."

"Oh, really? How many days?" She couldn't help the small frown on her face.

"Just a night, I think. I leave on Tuesday."

"Is it wrong that I already don't want you to leave?" She looked at him shyly, not sure if he was feeling the same way.

"Come with me."

Hannah scoffed. "Drew, you know I can't. I have Grace and the shop. I just can't take off on a whim."

"How were you able to leave for three days to work at Baton Timide?"

The question took her by surprise. Not his tone, the fact that he had wondered how she got the time off.

"One weekend a month, Grace goes and stays with Jackson's parents. I planned my first auction around that. I wasn't even sure I'd make it past the first auction, so I really hadn't planned on what would happen next."

He shook his head and a lopsided grin appeared. "Yes, well, we see how well that worked out. For me anyway." He brushed his lips lightly against hers.

"Yes, not too bad at all." She smiled.

"So, when does Grace go visit her grandparents again? Let's plan something then."

"Actually, it's next weekend. Sometimes they take her for Thanksgiving weekend because I get so busy at the shop, but now that she's getting older and will remember things, I told them I wanted her for the holiday."

"What about your family? You don't spend it with Tammy or your brother? Your mom and dad?"

She shook her head as sadness filled her eyes. "My mom and dad died in a car crash about six months after I married Jackson. I wasn't even pregnant then."

He pulled her closer into his arms and hugged her. "I'm really sorry. You never mentioned them, so I wasn't sure."

"It was really hard at the time. Jackson and Danny were both gone, and Tammy and I had to deal with everything. The funeral, packing up their house, trying to sell the house for enough to cover their mortgage. We discovered pretty quickly that neither one of them had been very good with money."

"I'm sure it was difficult."

"It was, but it's over now. I just wish they had gotten to meet Grace."

"You've had more than your fair share of loss. I'm really sorry."

She frowned. "I guess. But you have too. It's why it's so important to me that Grace sees Jackson's parents, and probably why I'm so protective of her. She's just a little girl. She deserves all the happiness and stability I can give her."

"Well, if it's too hard for you to get away, I certainly understand."

She looked up at him and smiled. "I'd like to go away with you. I really would. I just have to make sure the girls can cover the shop on Saturday."

Surprisingly, she was excited at the prospect of spending several days and nights with Drew. "What should we do?"

He smiled. "Do you want to go to my house on the shore? We can bring some food and just be hermits. Eat, sleep, have lots of sex. We could stay naked all weekend long."

His eyes grew dark at his own suggestion and before she could respond, he cupped her face and kissed her tenderly. "I don't care where we are or what we do. It will be nice to just spend some more time with you."

She leaned into his cheek and turned her head to kiss the soft spot in the center of his palm. "It sounds absolutely perfect, Drew."

"I'm exhausted, let's go to bed." Hannah rose up off of Drew.

Drew stood up next to her and pulled her into his arms. "Is it okay for me to stay?"

She tried to cover her mouth as it opened wide in a yawn. A small smile hit her lips. "As long as you let me sleep."

He kissed the tip of her nose and smacked her lightly on the ass before releasing her. "Done. I'm as tired as you."

They made their way to the bedroom, and Drew pulled off his T-shirt and jeans. With him in his boxers and her in a night-shirt, they both climbed into her bed, sliding under the covers and up against each other. Hannah rested her head on Drew's bare chest and listened to his heartbeat under her ear.

"Drew?"

"Hmmm." His fingers were tracing back and forth over her arm.

"Do you mind leaving before seven? That's when Grace usually wakes up. I just don't want to confuse her yet."

"Sure, no problem. I'm generally up much earlier than that."

She nodded her head on his chest and whispered, "Drew?"

"Yes?"

"I'm glad you're here."

Drew woke and tried to open his eyes but they were covered. Hannah's long hair was draped over his face. He was curled around her like a boa constrictor. He enjoyed the feel of her against his body, his cock twitching in agreement as it jutted against her backside. He brushed her hair out of the way and raised his wrist to look at the watch still strapped to it. It was just after five thirty a.m. Too early to wake her; she was exhausted.

He kissed the back of her head, savoring her floral scent as he did, and then slid out from under the covers. He grabbed his clothes and then carried them out to the bathroom so he could dress. He made a quick stop in the kitchen to drink a glass of water. He placed his empty water glass in the sink and then walked through the arch to the living room to grab his shoes.

He came to a screeching halt. Grace was sitting on the floor, coloring. He started to back up as quietly as he could but she swung her head up and saw him. A big wide grin broke across her face.

"Hi, Mr. Drew! Want to color with me?" She held the crayon in her hand up at him.

"Grace, what are you doing up so early?"

She shrugged, then wiped at her nose and started coloring again. "I woke up. But I saw you and Mommy sleeping so I came to color."

Shit. Hannah is going to freak. Oblivious to his own freak-out, Grace continued to color, concentration etching her forehead, her tongue peeking out of her mouth. He had a flash of his sister when she was young, her face scrunching up just like that when she was working something out. He wanted to scoop Grace up and give her a hug. Best not to push his luck.

"Gracie?" He spoke softly and her head swung up to look at him. "I've got to go. Will you be okay in here by yourself?"

He realized he was asking a four-year-old if she was okay to be alone and shook his head at his own stupidity. She stood up then, came over to him on her tiny feet and took his large hand in hers.

"Let's have some cereal. Mommy says we need breakfast every day."

He thought his heart would combust. Two girls were laying claim to his heart, not just one. He wrapped his large fingers around her small ones and let her lead him into the kitchen. She stopped in front of a pantry cupboard and used her free hand to pull the door open. She turned her head and looked up at him.

"Do you like Cheerios? Mommy won't buy me the Froot Loops." She stated it so matter-of-factly, making it clear that Froot Loops would obviously be the better choice. He nodded his head up and down.

"I do."

She let go of his hand then to pull the cereal out, then turned and put it down on the table. Then she walked over to a drawer and pulled out two spoons. She pointed to a cupboard up on the wall.

"Can you get the bowls, Mr. Drew?"

He jumped into action and did as she requested while she

walked over to the fridge to take out a carton of milk before meeting him back at the table. She scooted herself up into one of the chairs and sat up on her knees to pour some cereal in each of their bowls. He opened the milk and poured some in each bowl.

She lifted her spoon and brought it up over their bowls and looked at him expectantly. He wasn't sure what she wanted.

"Pick up your spoon and clink mine. That's what me and Mommy do."

He couldn't contain the grin that stretched across his face, and lifted his spoon and clinked it against hers. "Bon appétit!"

She scrunched her little nose up in confusion. "What's that mean?"

"It means I hope you enjoy your food."

Her lips creased into a little frown and she dipped her spoon into her cereal to take a bite. "Me and Mommy say cheers."

Drew chuckled at the defiance he was already so familiar with but wrapped up in this much more compact person. He lifted his spoon over his bowl and waited for Grace to tap his spoon again. "All right then. Cheers."

She smiled then and sat back on her knees as she continued to eat her Cheerios. He ate his bowl as well and watched in delight. Each time she chewed her food, she hummed at the same time. Neither one of them spoke as they ate, but instead just enjoyed the company of one another. When they were done, he was delightfully surprised as she took both bowls to the sink. She came back then and returned the milk to the fridge.

"You can go now if you want."

He chuckled at her bossy little nature. He didn't want to leave her alone if Hannah was still sleeping. He looked at his watch. It was a few minutes before six. He'd stay with Grace a bit longer and then wake Hannah up.

"Actually, I thought I'd color with you, if that's okay?"

She jumped up and down and clapped her hands together before clasping onto one of his to lead him into the living room. She pulled him down on the floor with her and reached for a coloring book from a stack beside her. She handed it to him with a big smile on her face.

"You can have Toy Story."

"Perfect."

She placed the box of crayons between them and returned to the picture she had previously been coloring. He watched her for a moment before pulling a brown crayon out of the box. He started working on a picture of a horse.

"That's Bullseye."

He looked down at the horse he was coloring and smiled. Grace chattered away as they completed their current pictures and started a new one.

"Hello." Hannah's tentative voice came from the doorway. Her hair was mussed, her eyes still sleepy. Grace popped up from her spot and ran to her mother, wrapping her arms around her legs in a hug.

"Mommy! You're awake!"

"Yes, and I see you are too. How come so early?" According to his watch, it was six thirty now.

Grace lifted her arms and shrugged. "I woke up."

He rose to his feet and walked over to Hannah, bending to place a tentative kiss on her cheek. "Good morning, beautiful."

Her cheeks turned a light pink as she glanced down at Grace, nodding her head in question. "Good morning?"

"She was up when I got up at five-thirty. I didn't want to leave her alone and I wanted to let you sleep."

Grace pulled on the hem of Hannah's T-shirt to get her attention. "Mommy, me and Mr. Drew had breakfast too."

He reached out to stroke Grace's hair. "Gracie you can just call me Drew. You don't have to call me mister."

Grace looked up at her mother for confirmation, who nodded. Grace chanted, "Drew, Drew, Drew. Just Drew."

Hannah sighed. "I need coffee."

He pulled her into the hallway. "I actually do need to go if you're up. Are we good? I'm really sorry Grace saw me. I was trying to sneak out."

"She seems totally fine with you being here." She shrugged. "Either my brain isn't awake yet, or I was being overly protective."

He looked down at the floor and then back up at Hannah, scratching his chin again. "Yeah, I think I'm just going to stay silent on this one."

Hannah's head was shaking in disbelief, but a slow smile spread across her face. "Welcome to my world, Drew. Single mothers who don't know if they are coming or going and who protect their babes like momma bears."

He took her face in his hands. "Like you said, we'll figure this all out. I just wanted to make sure you were okay with everything."

She nodded in his hands, and then he bent down to kiss her. She covered her mouth. "Morning breath."

He kissed her cheek instead. "I'll call you later.

CHAPTER TEN

A week later, Hannah waved goodbye to Grace one more time as Jackson's parents drove her away. They lived in one of the boroughs outside the city in a small Cape Cod style house with a large, fenced-in yard that sat on the edge of a field. They loved having Grace for any amount of time and she loved spending time with them as well. It was a way for both of them to keep their connection to Jackson alive.

Hannah looked down at her watch. Drew would be here any moment to pick her up. Her bags were packed and she had gone to the market at lunch and purchased groceries for them to bring as well. She was excited to spend two full days and two nights with Drew. They had only spent that much time together during their weekend at Baton Timide. Hopefully this time would end differently.

She turned to head back into her apartment when a black Mercedes SUV pulled into the alleyway. She stopped and waited as the door of the vehicle swung open and a jean-clad Drew stepped out. A smile graced her face and she closed the distance to greet him. He cupped her cheek as placed a kiss on her lips.

"Hello, gorgeous. I missed you."

She wrapped her arms around him as he pulled her in for a hug. "You just saw me yesterday."

"That's too long. You ready to go?"

She nodded. "So ready. All my stuff is in the hallway."

He released her and they walked to the door together to retrieve her things. He took her bags and coat, insisting he carry them all, and stood by the door while she locked up. He stowed her bags in the back of the SUV and then opened the passenger door for her.

"Is this your car too?"

"It's one of the hotel's. I thought it would be more comfortable than the Jag."

She shook her head as she climbed into the front seat. "Oh it's hard to be Andrew Sapphire."

He leaned into the car, then took her hand and placed it on his cock. It was hard and straining against his pants.

She looked up at him in surprise.

"Only every second I'm around you, Hannah Rose."

He released her hand and shut the door, securing her inside, before she could utter another word. He opened the driver door and slid in. "Buckle up, baby. You're in for a wild ride." He looked over at her with a devilish gleam in his eye.

She pulled her seatbelt over the shift dress she wore. She started when Drew placed his hand behind her neck and pulled her to him in a heated kiss. After several moments of tangled tongues, he broke the kiss and pulled out of the alley.

"Even one night away from you now is starting to feel too long."

She looked down at her hands in her lap, swooning. How can one sentence make me feel so wanted? Over the last week, he had come to her place for four of those nights. They seemed to be moving into an easy routine each evening. As good as it felt, she was still a little nervous to believe in happily ever after quite so soon.

When they were on the road, Drew rested his hand on

Hannah's leg. He inched up the hem of the dress up, resting his hand on her bare thigh. His need to feel her seemed to match her need for his touch. She squeezed his hand softly before entwining her fingers with his.

"I can't wait to spend the next couple days with you," she said.

"Me too. It's supposed to be stormy tomorrow. It will give us the perfect excuse to be lazy all day."

"I hope by lazy, you mean stay in bed."

His eyes met hers and the corners of his mouth rose. "Your wish is my command, princess."

Traffic was heavy given it was a Friday night, and they stopped for a light dinner on the way, so it was a little after nine by the time they arrived at his house. Hannah was impressed all over again by the high windows, clean lines and warm light that made up his home. He told her to go inside, giving her the security code to the door, as he retrieved all their belongings from the car.

She walked inside to the living room, remembering the meal they'd shared together after the masquerade ball, and a smile formed on her lips. She walked farther into the house and ran her fingers over Drew's stereo until she figured out how to turn it on and retrieve the playlists. When she found the one she wanted, she pressed play, turned the volume up loud and ran swiftly up the stairs and into his bedroom, leaving the room dark.

She raced over to the side of the bed and pulled her dress quickly over her head. She was wearing the necklace Drew had given her, and it bounced back down between her naked breasts as she dropped the dress on the floor. Next, she pulled off her shoes and slid her barely there panties off her body. She climbed up onto the bed and, before she lost her nerve, laid her body flat, raising her hands above her head and clasping them to the headboard. Then she waited.

The last time she had been in this room with Drew, things had started out like a dream and ended like a nightmare. She wanted to erase that night and create a new memory, a better memory for both of them. Was she doing the right thing, or was she pushing things too quickly?

The door slammed below, and then Drew called out to her. She didn't make a sound, but her breathing quickened in anticipation. She listened intently, trying to determine where he might be downstairs. He called for her again from what sounded like the library, and then his footsteps were on the stairs. Her heart beat wildly in her chest and she fought to keep her breathing controlled.

The door swung open and then Drew was silhouetted in the doorframe, illuminated by the light in the hallway. She waited, but he stood absolutely still. Finally, he slunk forward until he stood at the end of the bed.

"Holy fucking shit, Hannah." Drew's eyes roamed the length of Hannah's body laid out before him. She was offering herself to him like a sacrifice. He scrubbed his face to make sure he wasn't dreaming. From the bed, the delicate sounds of Hannah's voice reached his ears.

"I'm yours, Drew."

He couldn't contain the groan that tumbled out of his mouth as his cock throbbed to life inside his jeans. He reached down and ran his fingers down the inside of Hannah's leg, widening them further. Even with the low light from the hallway, he could see that her core was glistening. *How the fuck did I get this lucky? She is perfection.*

"Are you sure about this? This room doesn't have the best memories attached to it."

Her tongue darted out to wet her lips and she nodded. "I'm sure. I want to wash away all of that with something better."

He reached down and unbuckled his belt and then pulled it free from the loops. He stalked around the bed until he was standing at the head of it. "Do you trust me? Do you know I would never hurt you?"

Her head nodded up and down in the shadows.

"I need to hear you say it, Hannah."

"I trust you, Drew. Completely."

Without saying another word, he wove the belt around her wrists in a figure eight, then pulled it tight before securing it to the iron headboard. Her chest rose and fell quickly in response, the pulse at the base of her neck beating wildly and the nipples of her small, supple breasts peaking into hard beads. He stood there above her, wanting her to see and feel the desire he felt for her, as he released the buttons on his shirt, pulling it off and dropping it to the floor.

Her tongue peeked out of her mouth and wet her lips before darting back inside her mouth. He leaned down then and kissed her roughly, splaying his hands on each side of her head for traction. He pulled her tongue, her breath, her heat into his mouth and made it his own. He released her mouth, leaning back a fraction before running his own tongue around her lips. He leaned down and whispered, "Mine."

She nodded her head again and whispered back, "Yours."

His cock threatened to explode right then and there. She was his every fantasy come to life. He pushed himself off the bed and shucked his shoes and jeans. When he was free and naked, he leaned down again.

"What's your safe word?"

She blinked up at him in surprise. "Safe word?" She bit her lower lip and then spoke barely above a whisper. "Ghost. But Drew, the last time I used—"

He placed a finger over her lips to quiet her. "That will never happen again. Never. This is just to make sure I don't push you too hard."

She nodded and Drew took his finger away, dropping a chaste kiss there instead. He walked over to his dresser and pulled something out of the top drawer. He went to the end of the bed, grasped one of her ankles and pulled her down the bed until her arms were taught above her head. He looked at her for approval.

"Okay?"

"Yes," she breathed.

He chuckled and widened her leg, using a tie to secure the ankle to the corner of the bed frame. He moved to the other side and did the same thing with another tie. He walked to the head of the bed again and sat down next to her, leaning down so that his face was right above hers.

"Still okay?" "Yes," she panted.

The Dominant in him simmered. "Yes what?"

Hannah's eyes widened. "Yes, Sir."

"Don't forget again or I'll punish you."

"Yes, Sir." Not a moment of hesitation. She liked this just as much as he did.

Instead of moving away from her, he rose up over her body. Bracing his weight on his knees between her legs, he splayed his hands on each side of her head. Using his tongue, he started at her lips, tracing their outline before nipping the bottom one gently to pull on it. She yipped at the bite of pain and then licked the tender spot.

He took the opportunity to suck her tongue into his mouth until she was breathless. He released her mouth with a small pop and then trailed his tongue down her chin and to her ear. He ran it lightly over the lobe before brushing his lips against the tiny hairs and breathing hot and heavy into her. Her body surged upward, bumping into his, but he pushed it back down into the bed.

"You are so fucking perfect." It escaped his mouth on the lightest of breaths.

He trailed his tongue down her neck and then further, until he reached her breasts. Her skin was hot, the areola of her nipples dark and taut. He laved one of her nipples, the peak growing under his attention. He dragged his tongue, hard and flat, over it again and again until she fought her bindings, moans of desperation falling from her lips.

"Please, please," she whimpered.

"Please what? What do you want, Hannah?" Drew growled.

Hannah wiggled, her body in search of some kind of relief."More, I want more. Please . . . I need to feel you inside me."

Drew cooed, "Soon, my kitten, soon."

His cock wasn't throbbing, it was pounding, matching the drum beat of his heart, his balls drawn up tight and hard. He needed relief as much as she did, but not yet. He moved down her between her legs and used a finger to swipe between the lips of her pussy.

"Oh Jesus. You're so wet."

"Fuck me already," a frustrated Hannah mewled.

Drew pulled his hand back and slapped it lightly down on her clit. Hannah's hips bucked off the bed and a cry came from above.

"Fuck me already, Sir," Drew repeated.

Hannah's head was rocking back and forth as she dug her heels into the bed to try to push up into Drew. He clucked his tongue and slapped the inside of her thigh.

She yelped again but stilled, her body lying flat once more. Drew brought his mouth down to her core and ran his tongue up and down her pussy, sucking lightly at the juices that had built up. Moans were falling freely from Hannah's lips now and her hands were wrapped in a tight grip around the iron bed rail, her knuckles white.

He found her clit and began teasing it, flicking his tongue back and forth over the nub, increasing the pressure until he felt her core begin to tighten. Before she could come, he pulled back and ran his tongue down the length of her leg. Hannah cried out her frustration.

"Drew, please, please fuck me. I can't take anymore."

He knew he should punish her for using his name instead of "Sir" but he wasn't sure how much longer his cock could stand it either. He untied each of her ankles and then quickly covered her body with his, lining his cock up with her core, sliding his way home in one slow thrust.

They both moaned low at the action. Drew levered Hannah's knees up so he could drive deeper into her. He plunged into her again and again, each time slamming harder, pushing against her legs for traction. Amazingly, she took everything he gave her and begging for more.

"Harder, Drew, harder! I love when you fuck me like that!"

Drew's cock throbbed at her words and he slammed into her two more times before she begin clenching around him.

"Oh yes, yes, yes! Don't stop. Please don't stop!"

He didn't have to command her to come. He knew it was coming and as her pussy tightened in a final grip around his cock, he exploded his release into her in one last hard thrust, his hands clenching her knees as they yelled in unison. He held his cock deep inside her until she relaxed, and then pulled himself slowly out of her, releasing his hold on her limbs.

He got up on shaky legs and quickly unhooked the belt and her hands from the headboard. She lowered her arms, wincing in pain. Drew sat down beside her and massaged each one of her arms gently to restore blood flow to her muscles. She hummed her contentment as a small smile curved her lips.

He bent down and kissed her. It was soft and it was slow and it was full of love. God, I love this woman. The realization slammed into him like a truck, his heart stilling in his chest, his breath leaving him as he tore his lips from hers. Her eyes flew open.

"What is it?"

"Nothing. I'm okay." *I'm so fucked.*

He had told himself he wanted this, but did she love him back? Or did she just love fucking him? Everything between with them was still so tenuous.

She wrapped her arms around his neck and brought him back down to her. "More."

He shook his head in disbelief. "More? I think I'm done for a little while, you sexy minx." His heart had begun beating again, but his brain was still foggy as he responded to her on autopilot.

She smiled up at him sweetly. "Just more of those lips please."

He smiled back at her and submitted to her request, trailing kisses over her neck, face and finally her lips. After several moments, he broke away and lay down, pulling her into his arms. He needed some time to regroup his thoughts.

"Are you cold?" he asked.

"No. I'm perfect." She scooted even closer to him.

"Yes you are. And you're also full of surprises."

She pushed her face into his chest and mumbled, as if embarrassed by her omission. "I love when you tied me up at the bungalow."

Drew's cock actually twitched at her confession. No matter what his head might be thinking, his damn cock had a mind of its own. "What else did you like?"

She shook her head quickly. "No, no more. I'm too embarrassed as it is."

He looked down at her and couldn't keep the surprise from his voice. "Embarrassed about what? Do you know what you did to me when I walked in here and found you waiting for me, splayed out on my bed? My heart fucking stopped. Stopped. I wasn't sure if what you did at Baton was for the money or because you liked it. And I didn't want to push you."

She peeked up through her lashes, speaking quietly. "I liked everything you did to me, Drew. All of it. The spanking, tying me up, even you in my ass."

His breathing quickened as she spoke, not because he was excited, but because she was confirming again how much she liked having sex with him. But not a word was about how she felt about him. Because he didn't know what to say, he kissed her and then pulled her into his arms so he could hold her. It wasn't long before her breathing evened out in sleep. If only he could get his brain to shut down now.

Hannah woke slowly and rolled over, finding the bed empty except for her. She raised her arms above her head and stretched, feeling aches in all the right places.

She and Drew had made love once more during the night and had also gotten up around three for some water and a snack. She looked over at the clock on the nightstand. How was it almost eleven a.m.?

Feeling guilty for oversleeping and not checking in on Grace yet, she hopped out of bed to find her clothes and then her phone. She smiled when she noticed that Drew had left her bag on a stand outside the bathroom door. Sitting on top was her purse. She grabbed her phone and called Grace. After a ten-minute conversation filled with happy chatter about going to the zoo, she hung up. She threw her hair up in a tight bun before taking a quick shower.

After dressing and fixing her hair, she applied a light coat of lip gloss and left the bedroom to find Drew. As she reached the top of the stairs, she heard two male voices and wondered in surprise who might be here. Drew had told her that it would be just the two of them this weekend. She padded down the stairs and made her way into the kitchen.

Drew and his brother Ben were sitting at the bar. They both stopped talking when she entered the room, a wide smile breaking across Drew's features as he stood up and greeted her. He bent down and kissed her softly on the lips.

"Good morning, sleeping beauty." He turned and motioned toward Ben. "Look who decided to pop in for a surprise visit."

Ben stood up as well. He wasn't using a cane this time; was it more for show than for purpose? It wasn't a subject she would broach with him, especially after their last shaky encounter. He was standing in front of her now and nodded his head in greeting.

"Hannah?" He said like a question.

Her forehead scrunched in confusion, but then it clicked. She had originally been introduced to Ben as Scarlett. Had Drew told

Ben how they had actually met? *Oh lord, how am I going to explain this one?*

She leaned forward and surprised him by pecking him on his cheek. "Ben. Nice to see you again."

He tilted his head and looked at her for a moment. "I feel like this is the first time we've met, actually. Drew hasn't told me everything except that you're Hannah, not Scarlett. But you were Scarlett."

"Scarlett O'Hara, for the masquerade ball." She replied quickly, not even sure how she had just pulled that out of her ass. Drew's eyebrows shot up at her quick response, and then he nodded in approval. Ben, however, continued to scrutinize her.

Drew stepped between them and put an arm around her, maneuvering her to the table to sit. "Are you hungry, Hannah? Coffee maybe?"

She could feel Ben's eyes on her as she sat in the chair Drew pulled out for her, but she tried to act unaffected. "Yes, coffee would be lovely."

"Coming up." Drew pulled a mug down from the cupboard before popping a coffee pod into the brewer. When it was done, he took the peppermint mocha creamer she had brought and poured some into her cup, stirring it before placing it in front of her. As he did, he brushed a kiss against the top of her forehead and sat beside her. Ben had already grabbed a cup of coffee off the bar, where he and Drew had been talking, and sat across from her at the table.

She turned toward Drew and placed her hand over his. "What time did you get up?"

"I think around seven. The rain hadn't started yet so I went for a run down the beach for about an hour. When I came back, I found a message from Benny, saying he was coming out for the day."

"Sorry, I didn't realize Drew would have company. That hasn't been an issue for a long time."

I'm an issue? She shrugged off his comment and nodded instead.

"No worries. We were just planning to sit around and be lazy anyway."

She hoped Drew wouldn't bring up that their definition of lazy involved a bed, but he gave her a knowing smile and kept silent. He took her hand instead and raised it to his lips, turning it to kiss her palm.

"Ben wanted to get out of the city for a few days and my secretary told him I'd come out to the house, so he headed out early this morning to beat any traffic."

A couple days? He's staying? So much for being naked and alone all weekend. She nodded and took a sip of her coffee. Ben stared at her intently. "Is something wrong?"

His forehead creased. "Sorry, I don't mean to stare. I feel like we've met before. Like I know you from somewhere."

"Well, we met at the ball. I was wearing a mask, so maybe it just feels different seeing my whole face?"

He shook his head. "No. It's not that. It will come to me. Or maybe it's nothing. My head got banged up pretty good in my accident."

Drew punched his brother lightly on the arm. "Your head was screwed up way before that accident, Brother."

Ben snorted. "Fuck you." Then he whipped his head back to Hannah. "Sorry. Shouldn't swear like that in front of a lady. It's the soldier in me."

Hannah smiled, understanding better than he could have realized. "No apologies. My brother was in the army. Every other word out of his mouth is foul. I practically need to wash his mouth out with soap when he's with Grace."

He tilted his head. "Who's Grace?"

She hesitated for a moment. This was new territory for her. This was her first serious relationship since Jackson and she hadn't ever had to explain her situation before. Before she could speak, Drew did.

"Grace is her daughter. She's almost five. She is a beautiful, precocious clone of her mother."

Ben looked at Drew, surprise evident on his face, before turning back at Hannah. "She with her dad this weekend?"

It was an innocent enough question, but one that caused her face to heat and her heart to pick up its pace.

"She's with her grand—" "Hannah's a wid—"

So much for the simple answer. She looked at Drew, her expression turning angry, even though it made no sense to feel that way. This was her information to share if she wanted, not his.

Before she could say anything, Ben spoke quietly. "I'm sorry, Hannah. Truly."

His genuine sorrow at her loss cooled her anger and also made her feel that perhaps she had been too quick to judge Ben.

"Was he military? Overseas? That's why you got so angry at me when I showed you my leg at the ball. Isn't it?"

Hannah was surprised he'd put the very few exposed pieces of her life together so quickly, but she nodded. "Yes. And yes. And yes."

He reached across the table then to place a hand over hers, his shirtsleeve stretching up and exposing a forearm covered in tattoos. But the one that caught her attention again was the black rose with a gold leaf cluster that started at the base of his wrist and wound a few inches up his forearm. That damn tattoo.

Without any warning, she jumped up and pushed his shirtsleeve higher, exposing the words "Never Forget", just like she knew would be there.

Both Drew and Ben looked at her, surprise on both of their faces. Drew spoke first. "Hannah, what are you doing?"

Her body chilled as the blood drained from it. Her hands shook as she pointed at the tattoo. "Why do you have that?"

Ben looked up at her and then down at the tattoo, and as if lightning had struck, his expression changed to one of comprehension. "Holy Fuck. You're Jackson's Hannah and Grace. You're Danny's sister."

CHAPTER ELEVEN

"How do you know Jackson and Danny?" Hannah felt stupid for even asking the question. It was obvious they must have served together. "And why do you have that tattoo? Danny has the same tattoo over his heart. He got it to honor Jackson after he was killed."

Ben stared at her wide-eyed, apparently still in shock at his own discovery, before looking down and running his finger over the tattoo. "I served with them both in Iraq. Jackson and I were in the same unit. We were together in the Humvee when we struck that IED."

Hannah pushed her chair back and started pacing, wringing her hands together as she tried to put the new pieces of this puzzle together. She spun back around and threw her hands up in the air. "How come I never met you? All of Jackson's unit came to his funeral. And Danny's never mentioned you."

Ben glanced down at his leg and then back at up her. "I should have come to the funeral. I should have. I'm sorry. I just couldn't see beyond myself and my own pain then. I was still in the hospital when I heard that Black Jack—" He looked up at her again and frowned. "Sorry, that's what we all called him. He won enough money beating us at poker to feed half a country."

He laughed then. The hollow sound just stoked her anger higher. She shook her head as if it to clear the emotions swirling in it. Drew stood up from his chair and tried to wrap his arms around her, but she shrugged him away.

He reeled back, surprise etched on his face. "Hannah, I just want to help."

She looked at him in astonishment. "Just how do you think you're going to help me, Drew? You think a hug is going to make this all right?"

Drew gripped one of her hands. "I don't understand why you're so upset. Isn't it a good thing if you found someone who knew your husband and can share things with you about him?"

She shook her head again and let out a small disgusted laugh before looking at Drew. "You really don't get it, do you?"

She wrenched her hand away from Drew's grasp and stormed over to where Ben was still sitting, eyes downcast.

"You know why I'm mad, don't you Ben?"

He pushed his chair back and stood, then sighed, "You think it's my fault he got killed."

She shoved his chest with both hands as she yelled, "It is your fault!"

Ben took two stumbling steps backward and looked like he was going to lose his balance, but grabbed the back of a chair, righting himself before falling. At the same time, Drew reached out and pulled her back and away from Ben, but she twisted free and turned to glare at him.

"Don't, Drew."

"Hannah, you're angry. I get it. Sit down so we can discuss this more calmly."

She scoffed, raking her hands through her hair in frustration. "I don't want to be calm, Drew. I'm pissed. Don't you get it? If your darling brother hadn't made my husband feel guilty for not being injured, he would still be here with me today. My daughter would have a father. The man I love would still be here and my life would be perfect."

As soon as the words left her mouth, a look of such hurt and devastation crossed Drew's face, instantly fueling her with regret. She didn't want to hurt Drew. She cared deeply about him too. She took a quick step forward and pulled his hand into both of hers. "Drew, I'm sorry. I didn't mean it like that."

Drew stood before her, his head tilted, eyes crinkled in his examination of her, as if he wasn't sure who she was. He slipped his hand out from between hers. He took two steps back away from her, still silent, still staring at her. Her anger at Ben was temporarily forgotten as panic rose up and claimed her nerves.

"Drew, please. Don't look at me like that." She took two steps toward him to gain the ground she had lost, but he countered again and just shook his head, holding a palm out flat. She raised her hands up to her side, palms up, trying to open herself up to him. Seeing him look at her like this and knowing she could lose him made her realize just how much she had come to care for him. *Am I in love with him?*

She stepped toward him again, more confused than ever. "I'm sorry. I'm so sorry. I lost my temper."

"Hannah—" he started, but then he exhaled, rubbing at the stubble on his chin. "Hannah, just stop for a minute."

She cocked her head to the side. "Stop?"

"Yes, stop. Stop yelling, stop making assumptions. Just let Ben talk, for Christ's sake."

The words were like gasoline on the banked flame of her anger. "Let Ben talk?"

Her voice dripped with sarcasm before turning quieter. "He's had over two years to come and talk to me. Two years. Why didn't he?"

"Hannah, don't you thin—"

"She's right." Ben spoke firmly.

Both she and Drew gawked at him. Ben met her gaze. "You're right."

He let go of the chair and took a couple steps closer. His voice stayed firm, but it was low and apologetic. "I should have come to see you. A long time ago. Maybe I could have saved you some of the pain you still feel."

Tears started to roll in slow trails down her cheeks. She smiled wryly through them. "I'm always going to feel that pain. You can't fix that."

She brushed aside the tears, angry for letting them fall at all. A small, sardonic grin fell on her lips and she shook her head before addressing Ben again. "You got the last of him. You know that?"

His eyebrows furrowed in confusion.

"He went to see you every day in that hospital when he came home for the funerals. He spent every day with you. Grace was less than a year old, and it was as if she didn't exist for him anymore. He barely came home, and when he did, he wouldn't even look at me. He gave everything he had left, to you. After that, he gave everything to his men. And I have nothing."

She wasn't yelling anymore; she was just sad. Sad that this man was the reason her husband was dead. Sad that Jackson had chosen this man over her. And even sadder that he was Drew's brother. There was no way to escape him and the feelings he exposed if she wanted to stay with Drew.

At this last thought, she turned and looked at Drew, utter grief engulfing her. "I want to go home."

She turned and before either of the men could say a word, she ran from the room and up the stairs to the bedroom. She grabbed her bag and flung it on the bed, quickly stuffing her belongings into it. Just as she zipped it up, the bedroom door flew open and Drew stalked in, his face pinched and hard.

"Hannah, what the fuck are you doing?" He grabbed each of her arms, turning her toward him.

She hung limply in his grasp, all strength having left her system when she understood what she needed to do.

"I'm leaving. Can I take your car? Can you go back with your brother?" She didn't even want to say his name.

He bent down so that his face was even with hers. "What do you mean, you're leaving?"

Her head swung back and forth, her hair swishing over her shoulders from the motion. "I have to go. I can't stay here. This is all wrong now."

His grip around her arms tightened, but she didn't fight him. She deserved this for what she was about to do to him.

"I can't be with you, Drew. Not after this. I will never be able share a place with your brother, and I won't make you choose between us."

"Hannah, no!" He shook her lightly and then pulled her body against his, wrapping his arms around her tightly. She didn't reciprocate. She left her arms dangling loosely by her side. If she reached around and hugged him, she wouldn't be able to let go.

His breath was hot against her ear as he pleaded with her. "I just got you back. I'm not losing you again. We can figure this out."

She squeezed her arms up between them and pushed out of his hold. Tears were rolling freely down her cheeks, leaving large wet droplets on her sweater. Pieces of her hair were stuck to her face where Drew had hugged her, but she made no motion to wipe them away. "Please, just let me go. It's too much."

"It's not too much. Let me talk to Ben. He can leave. You and I will figure this out. Please, Hannah."

She turned away and grabbed her bag off the bed. He tried to pull it away from her, but she held on firmly and looked up at him pleadingly. "Please . . . please don't make this any harder for me. I can't be with you."

Her words finally seemed to sink in as Drew let go of the bag and staggered back two steps, his face pale, his mouth open in shock.

Before she could change her mind and before Drew could try and stop her again, she ran out of the room and down the stairs. She found the Mercedes's key hanging on a hook by the front door and grabbed it as she escaped out into the rain and sleet.

Drew watched her run out of the bedroom and felt his knees give out from under him as he fell back onto the bed. This bedroom was like a goddamn curse. Every time she left him, it was in this fucking room. He had an urge to burn the house down so he could remove it from the equation, but when he heard the front door slam shut, he bolted up. All thoughts about the house vanished.

Was she actually going to leave? His question was answered when the engine of a car roared to life, making him sprint out the room and down the stairs. He flung open the front door and ran down the driveway, watching as the Mercedes pulled out into the street and sped away.

"Fuck!" He kicked at the loose gravel and threw his hands up in the air, screaming again. "God damn fucking fuck!"

He spun around and stormed back into the house, slamming the front door behind him so hard the glass rattled in its pane. He stomped toward the kitchen. "Ben? Where the fuck are you?"

He spun around as a voice called out from behind him. "Upstairs."

Drew took the stairs two at a time and walked down the hallway to the guest bedroom. The door was open and Ben was moving his stuff from the dresser into a small duffel. "I'm leaving, don't worry."

"Good, I'm going with you. Hannah took my car."

He turned to leave the room so he could grab what few things he had brought with him, but Ben's hand stopped him. He twisted back around to look at his brother. "What?" Impatience dripped from his voice.

Ben dropped his hand from his arm. "I'm sorry. I don't know what the fuck just happened."

"The woman I'm in love with just left me. That's what the fuck just happened."

Ben shifted, transferring his weight to his good leg. "You love her?"

Drew's eyes lowered. He had actually said it out loud. "Yeah, I guess I do."

"Okay. I'll be ready in five minutes."

"Good. I just have to grab a couple things and I'll meet you downstairs."

Fifteen minutes later, Drew and Ben had locked up the house, loaded their bags into the trunk of the car and were backing into the street. The weather was shitty. It was sleeting more than it was raining and he hoped that Hannah was driving carefully. He was thankful she was in the more solid SUV, not the Jaguar he'd left in Manhattan.

He pulled out his cell and tried to call her, but after two rings it went to voicemail. That goddamn stubborn woman had just declined his call. He didn't want her to text and drive but he also wanted her to know he wasn't letting her slip out of his grasp that easily. He sent a quick message.

On my way to you.

The message was received and then read, but after several minutes with no reply back, he put the phone in his pocket with a sigh of frustration. In the driver's seat, Ben stared intently ahead.

"Did you know?"

Ben turned to him for a second, eyes dark, before looking back at the road. "Know what?"

"Did you know who she was?"

Ben shook his head and huffed. "Seriously, Drew? What kind of person do you take me for? Of course I didn't know. Not until she asked about the tattoo. Not until she said her brother had one did the pieces click together. Only three of us got this tattoo. Me, Danny and Tyler. And Tyler lives in California."

Drew nodded in understanding but still needed more answers. Not only for himself, but for Hannah. "Why didn't you go see her? She's right, you know. It's been over two years since your accident."

Ben's knuckles tightened around the steering wheel and his breathing increased. He was silent for several long minutes before he spoke. "You know what it was like for me. When they made the decision to take my leg."

Ben's grip loosened and then his hands stretched out flat as he banged them several times on the top of the wheel.

"When I found out Jack had been killed, I felt like I was in that explosion all over again. And I felt like a failure. I couldn't even get out of bed without help, could barely take a piss without getting it all over myself. I was a fucking mess. I felt so goddamn helpless. And angry. Angry that I wasn't there to help him. Angry that I was still alive and everyone else kept fucking dying without me."

Drew remembered that time well. He'd gone to visit Ben in the hospital almost every day after they'd taken his leg, and every visit had been hell. Ben wouldn't talk to him, and he had refused to speak to anyone that would help him. Things had been really dark for a long time. So dark that no one had been that surprised when Ben took a bottle of Vicodin one night.

He had already lost one sibling, and he thanked God every day that Ben hadn't died. Something had changed in him after that and he'd slowly emerged from the dark place he'd been in and begun quietly learning how to live again with his new body.

"I remember, Ben."

"I couldn't help her then. And when I was finally feeling whole again, it felt like too much time had passed, and I couldn't bring myself to go and see her. I figured she would have moved on by then and I didn't want to make things harder on her. Danny said she was doing okay, and I believed him."

Drew studied him intently for a moment before challenging him. "You mean, you didn't want to make things any harder on you by going to see her."

Ben's grip clenched and unclenched around the steering wheel a few times before he finally responded. "Maybe, maybe. But I'm telling you right now, I never told Jack to go back. Never. I told him to stay."

The rest of the drive was spent in tense silence. Drew tried calling Hannah several more times, but each time he went straight to voicemail. The traffic going back into the city was almost nonexistent due to the weather, and Ben's confident driving had them back in under two hours.

"Do you want to go to the hotel?"

"No, take me to her place. It's on Third, closer to Thirty-Ninth Street."

Ben turned the car in that direction. Drew told him to pull into the alley when they reached her shop several moments later. Her van was there, but he didn't see the Mercedes. It was just before three, so the shop was still open. He opened the car door, stepped out, then bent down. "Wait here."

He walked into the shop, the familiar bell tinkling as the door pulled open, and looked around. No one. "Hello?"

As soon as he called out, a woman appeared from the doorway at the back of the shop. He recognized her as the woman who had walked in on him and Hannah the day he had finally confronted her. She walked toward him, and recognition crossed her features as she got closer. Then her brows creased in question.

"What are you doing here? Aren't you and Hannah supposed to be in the Hamptons?"

Drew ignored her question and asked his own instead. "So, Hannah's not here?"

"Um, no. I thought she was with you." She put her hands on her hips, attitude starting to make its way into her posture. "Did you do something to Hannah?"

He sighed in frustration. "Listen, just tell her I came by and to call me."

Without waiting for her to respond and dreading the possibility of the third degree, he turned and left as abruptly as he had entered, running back to Ben's waiting car.

"Was she there?"

"Nope. Maybe she stopped somewhere?"

Ben shrugged. "Maybe."

"Let's just go to the hotel. I'll come back later if I don't hear from her soon."

Ben backed the car out of the alley and made it back to the hotel in ten minutes. They pulled up to the valet and put the car in park. "You want me to come in with you?"

Drew stared out the windshield. "Look, it's the Mercedes. She's here."

He jumped out of the car and flew into the hotel, looking for the valet. He found him just inside, one of the regulars Drew knew by name.

"Mr. Sapphire. Welcome back. Bad weather bring you back early?"

"Bobby, hi. The SUV outside? Where did the woman go that was driving it?"

Bobby's face broke out in a grin as he walked over to the valet desk. "Oh yes, sir. The woman that dropped it off said to give these keys to you when you returned. She didn't stay though. I put her in a cab."

"A cab?" *Shit, she's not here.*

"Yes, sir."

"Did you get the address where she was going?"

Bobby shook his head. "No, sir. She didn't give me one. I'm sorry."

"How long ago?"

Bobby pulled up the sleeve of his coat to look at his watch. "Maybe fifteen minutes ago?"

"Fuck!"

Bobby shrank back at Drew's outburst. "I'm sorry, sir."

Drew ran a frustrated hand through his hair. "No, no, it's not your fault. Thank you."

Ben was walking into the hotel then, Drew's bag in hand. They met midway and Ben handed over the bag. "Anything?"

He scowled. "Nope. She dropped off the car about fifteen minutes ago and left in a cab. Not sure where."

"Back to the shop?"

"I don't know. I'll go back there in a little bit if she doesn't answer my call."

Ben clapped him on the shoulder. "You going to be okay?"

Drew looked at his brother and nodded. "I will be. As soon asI find her."

Where the fuck was she?

CHAPTER TWELVE

Hannah climbed into the back of the cab and told the driver to just drive. She didn't want to go back to the shop or the apartment for fear that Drew would come looking for her. She wasn't expected back at the shop until Monday, so she had two days to try and pull herself together. She looked down at her phone again as it buzzed. Drew trying to reach her again. She hit the decline button and wiped away the stray tear falling from her eye.

"Do you have somewhere you want to go, miss?"

"Can you just drive for a little bit? Maybe through the park?"

The driver nodded in acknowledgement.

"Thank you."

She didn't know where to go. For the thousandth time since she'd left Drew's house, she wondered what the hell had happened. How? How was it possible that out of the million men in Manhattan, she'd gone and fallen in love with the one man whose brother was the reason her husband was dead? And she loved Drew. It took her having to walk away from him to realize it, but she did. She loved him. But she also knew seeing Ben would be a constant reminder of her husband's loss.

How did she balance the two? She didn't know how. And she absolutely refused to make Drew choose between her and his brother. She knew how much his brother meant to him, especially after already losing his sister. She had lived without his love before and would survive this and manage to do it again. That thought squeezed her heart and a small sob escaped her throat.

This is why she shouldn't have opened herself up to love again. In the end, there was always just so much pain. She rested her head against the cool glass of the window and watched the scenery in the park slide by. Even in the rain, people were out jogging and walking hand in hand with loved ones, huddled together under umbrellas. She ached, knowing she had lost the very thing she had feared most, but ultimately found anyway.

They had been driving around the park in circles for about forty minutes when the driver spoke again. "Miss, you're at forty dollars. Do you want to keep driving?"

They were near the center of the park. Light rain was still falling. "I'll get out here please."

The car slowed and came to a stop at the side of the road. She handed the driver a fifty and told him to keep the change, taking her bag and moving to leave the car.

"You going to be okay?" He was an older gentleman and had probably seen his fair share of women crying in the back of his cab before, but his concern was no less sincere.

She nodded, grateful. "Yes, I'll be okay, thank you."

He just nodded in return and turned back around in his seat. She shut the door and gripped her bag tightly in one hand as she began to walk through the park. She was wearing a peacoat without a hood, her face and hair bare to the fine mist. She didn't mind. The cool air was refreshing on her warm, tear-streaked face.

Her mind wandered as she walked and she thought back on her time with Drew. From her first stolen glimpse of him from the stage at Baton Timide, to walking on the beach outside his lovely home. From dancing in his living room, to just lying in his arms less than twelve hours before. How quickly life could change. She knew that, of course. After losing Jackson, she knew how unpredictable and unfair life could be.

Ben. He was the one. The one that had stolen the last bit of time she'd had with Jackson. The one who'd made him go back and avenge the deaths of their lost friends. The one who'd ripped her life away. What would life with Jackson be like if he had never gone back to Iraq? It was strange. When she thought of her future now, she could only picture Drew.

Exhaustion overwhelmed her as she reached the edge of the park and made her way out to the street. A bench sat against the high stone wall that surrounded the park, and even though it was sopping wet, she collapsed onto it. She shifted her bag to her lap, clutching it like a life preserver. She stared ahead at nothing, unable to process anything more. The sky was darkening. Would anyone mind if she just stayed here on this bench for the night?

D rew paced back and forth in his suite at the hotel, his pulse in overdrive at not being able to find Hannah.

He had called her several more times, leaving messages pleading for her to call him, and had also gone back to the shop, but to no avail. Telling Drew to call him if he could help, Ben had gone back to his place about an hour ago .

Not sure what else to do with his restless energy, he went down to his office to see if he could find something to keep his mind busy. Instead of taking the elevator, he took the stairs, emerging into a very empty office space. It was late on a Saturday, and the few people that may have come in for the day were long gone.

He walked into his office, choosing not to turn on the overhead lights, and sat in his chair in the dark. He checked his phone again, just in case. Still nothing. He spun around and let his gaze wander outside. It was still raining, and people darted in and out of cabs, or walked hurriedly down the sidewalk, scrunched under umbrellas, the collars of their jackets turned up high to keep dry. His eyes drifted to a lone person sitting on a bench next to the entrance to the park. His heart stilled. She was sitting there, clutching her bag, wet hair falling forward over her bowed head. Hannah.

He jumped out of his chair and ran for the elevator, punching the call button furiously, willing it to come more quickly. The elevator finally dinged, announcing its arrival, and then the doors slid open. He stepped in and hit the button for the lobby, praying it didn't stop at any other floors on the way down. When it finally came to a stop, he surged through the doors as they slid free and he ran to the side exit of the hotel that faced the park.

She was still sitting there in the same exact position. He looked both ways, checking the street before racing across, dodging an oncoming car, its horn blaring, and reaching the other side. He knelt down in front of her on the bench. Her whole body was shivering and she was soaked from head to toe. He touched her knees through her wet jeans.

"Hannah?" He kept his voice soft and gentle, as if he were speaking to a child. Tears were running from her eyes, but she didn't move, nor did she speak. He brought his hands up to her arms and shook her gently. "Hannah?"

This time her eyes did move, but when she tried to speak, gibberish poured from her lips. At a loss, he scooped her up in his arms. She fell into him like a limp noodle, whimpering dully. He strode back across the street and into the lobby of the hotel.

George was suddenly rushing up in front of him, concern etching his features. "Mr. Sapphire? Is that Hannah? What happened? What can I do to help?"

He didn't slow down, walking past George and toward the elevator. "George, can you just put the security code in for my apartment? My hands are kind of full."

His arms were starting to ache. George scurried in behind him on the elevator and quickly typed in the code for Drew's suite. He backed out again before the doors could close and tipped his head at Hannah.

"Just call me if you need anything at all."

Drew thanked him as the door slid closed and the elevator

started its ascent. Hannah was shivering furiously in his arms, her head lolling up against his chest each time he moved, but she still hadn't said a single word. When the doors slid open, he walked straight through the suite and into his bedroom, gently setting her down on the bed. She remained in a sitting position, but her head hung as limp as her wet, tangled hair.

He unbuttoned her coat and slid it off her. It had been useless against the rain, and her sweater underneath was as wet as the rest of her. How long was she sitting out there? He continued to undress her, then scooped her naked body up in his arms again and walked to the bathroom.

He turned on the water in the shower and waited for it to get hot, then stepped in, holding Hannah close to him in his arms. He was still fully clothed, but his only concern at the moment was getting her warm. When the hot water hit her skin, she cried out like she had been whipped and curled her body further into his.

"Shhh, Hannah. I need to warm you up." He spoke softly into her ear and set her down on the bench seat at the end of the shower. He turned on the manual shower head and moved it over her hair and skin. He reached for a sponge on the ledge and used it to rub her skin in small circles, trying to get her circulation moving again. She moaned and her head fell back against the tile, her eyes closing tightly.

He continued to speak quietly, trying to comfort and assure her she would be okay. When her body had turned back to a normal pink and its touch was warm again, he shut the water off. He pulled a large towel off the rack and wrapped it around her. Before stepping out of the shower, he peeled off his wet clothes and left them in a pile. He grabbed another towel and wrapped it tightly around his waist before moving back to Hannah.

He scooped her up again and carried her back to his bed. He reached down and awkwardly pulled back the covers before sliding her in between them. He laid her down flat and pulled the damp towel from around her body before pulling the covers tight around her. He walked around to the other side of the bed and dropped the towel from his waist before sliding in next to her, wrapping his arms around her and pulling her close.

She didn't resist. She melted into him as a soft whimper left her. His heart broke into a million pieces for the pain she was feeling. Everything he wanted was right here in his arms, yet she was so far away. He would fix this. If it was the last thing he did, he would make her realize that their love could conquer anything.

W*hy am I so hot?* She tried to roll over but found herself wrapped up tight in a pair of strong arms and legs. Her eyes shot open as she remembered the hazy events of the night before.

Rain, wet and cold. Drew lifting her up. Hot, burning streams of water pinging her skin and then circles of softness warming her. Covers sliding over her and then heat, hot and pliant against her skin before she fell unconscious. She had somehow ended up in his arms, in his bed.

She tried to pull herself out of his embrace, but he moaned and tightened his hold on her. His head nuzzled into the back of her head and she felt his breath, hot and steady before his lips pressed against the back of her neck.

"You're not leaving," he crooned against her neck, the vibration of his lips raising goose bumps across her body. He continued kissing her neck, brushing his nose against her hair to nudge it out of the way and then moving his lips back again.

"Drew, stop," she protested, but her body betrayed her and rocked back against him, her core already throbbing at the simple pleasure his lips brought her.

One arm loosened around her center and trailed up her side. His hand cupped her breast and slowly caressed it, his fingers plucking her nipple as it hardened.

She let out a soft sigh and gave in to his touch. As her body relaxed, his hold around her slackened. He pushed his hard

member up against the cleft in her ass, never stopping his atten-
tions to her breast or the small kisses he kept raining on her neck,
her shoulders, her back. She arched into him and wrapped an
around his head, turning back to meet his lips with hers.

He kissed her then. Torturously slow, his lips brushed against
hers with the lightest touch, his tongue tracing the outline of her
lips and then sliding inside to tease. She surged forward, fusing
their lips together, wanting to taste all of him. She inhaled deeply,
taking his breath into her as if she needed it to survive.

His hand clasped her face, holding her to him, while the other
one adjusted his cock behind her and then slid it into her wet
pussy. A moan rolled out of her mouth and into his as he thrust
forward, and she fisted his hair. He released his hold on her breast
and slid down between her legs until he found the hard hood of
her clit. She bucked as he slid his finger against it, his dick slamming into her harder.

He rubbed her clit back and forth, his finger in sync with his
cock thrusting in and out of her. With each stroke, his cock
throbbed larger inside her. His mouth was against her ear and his
breath was heated as he began whispering.

"I'm never letting you go, Hannah. Ever. You're mine. I own
you. I own your body. I own your love."

He drove into her harder then and her body began the familiar
climb toward orgasm he brought her to every time. Her only
response was to nod frantically as she felt herself getting ready to
detonate.

On the next thrust, he pinched her clit between his fingers and
she shattered into a tiny million particles of light. Her body tightened and she chanted, "Yours, yours, yours," over and over again.
Then Drew's release burst inside of her, and his grip around her
tightened before he let out one more strangled word: "Mine."

As she came down from the high his touch gave her, reality
washed over her like a bucket of cold water. He was trying to pull
her snug against him again, but this time she wrestled free and sat
up. She turned to face him and the look of shock on his face.

"I should go. This shouldn't have happened. I'm sorry."

His expression morphed to one of anger as he sat up as well. "No. We are not doing this again."

She closed her eyes, trying to force her heart to stop beating so wildly, and then looked at him again. She brushed a loose strand of hair across his eyes back against his forehead.

"Drew, this didn't change anything that happened yesterday. This situation is just too much."

He took her hand in his and pressed it flat against his chest over his heart. "Do you feel this?"

She could feel the strong pulse of his heart under her hand and nodded. "Yes."

"It beats only for you now. If you leave, if you go, I don't know how to keep it beating, how to keep breathing."

"Drew, please," she pled, drawing her hand away. "Please don't make me do this all over again."

His voice grew firm. "Then don't. I love you."

Her body stiffened at his words. "What?"

"I'm in love with you. And I think you love me too."

Instant denial forced her lips into a frown. "It doesn't matter anymore. Ben is your brother. And I can't make you walk away from him. I can't. He's your brother. You've only known me three months."

Drew raked his hand through his hair. "I'll keep you two apart. Or we'll talk together and figure this out. He said he didn't ask your husband to go back."

Her pulse raced again. "What?"

"I don't know. He just told me that he didn't ask him to go back."

Hannah let out a deep sigh and stood. "This is all just too weird. Of all the people I could have ended up with, and then to find out about this connection your brother has to my husband."

"He's gone, Hannah. You have to move forward." His tone was hardening with anger.

"How can I move forward if every time I see you, I think of

Ben, and then I think of Jackson and that maybe he should be here instead? That's not fair to you!"

Drew's head dropped into his hands and he growled in frustration. "Goddamn it, Hannah. How many more excuses are you going to find to push yourself away from me? First it's your daughter, then I spend too much on you, then I treat you too much like a sub, and now it's your dead husband."

Time to move this along. Where were her clothes? She saw her jeans and rose to pull them out of the damp heap beside the bed.

Drew jumped out of the bed and yanked the jeans out of her hands. "You are not running away again. If I have to lock you up and keep you here, I will."

She tugged at the sodden denim in his grasp. "Fuck you. You can't keep me prisoner. Give me my damn pants."

"No."

She looked at him, so angry she could scream, and stalked around him. She jerked open drawers in his dresser until she found what she was looking for. She pulled out a pair of sweats pants and threw them on before he could stop her. Her hands were shaking as she pulled out a T-shirt next. "Who the fuck do you think you are, Drew? You think you can tell me what to do? How I choose to live my life?"

He dropped her jeans on the floor and parked in front of her. "I am the man that's in love with you. I'm telling you not to throw this away because you're scared. I want you to choose to live your life with me. I love you, Hannah. I want to spend the rest of my life with you. With Grace. Maybe make another little Grace. Don't you get that? You own me."

She stilled, every frantic muscle in her body frozen in astonishment. "What?"

He took her face into his hands and pulled her close. "I love you so much it fucking hurts. I can't imagine my world without you in it now."

Anger taking over, she wrenched away from him, looking around the room. *Where the fuck where her shoes?* "I can't believe you're going to say this to me now. Now! Why not two days ago? Before you thought you were going to lose me? I can't hear your words of desperation. I can't believe them."

She found her wet shoes and bag and grabbed them as she dashed to the elevator.

"Hannah, stop."

"Stop?" she replied sarcastically as she mashed the elevator button.

Drew stomped after her. "Yes, stop. Stop being scared. Stop being so angry. Stop loving Jackson. Please."

The elevator dinged and the doors slid open. She stepped inside, Drew coming to a halt at the threshold.

"Fuck you, Drew."

CHAPTER THIRTEEN

Drew dropped to his knees, his fist punching the door, his heart plummeting to the ground with the elevator. He realized as his bare knees slammed against the cold marble that he was still naked.

He'd thought he had her back when she didn't resist him this morning, but he had only been fooling himself. And now she was gone and he had no idea how he was going to get her back again. She truly believed this couldn't be fixed, but he would find a way. It wasn't going to happen on his knees though, so he pushed himself up and walked back into the bedroom.

He found his phone and dialed. It rang only once before Ben's strong voice answered. "Drew."

"Can I come over?"

"I'm in the middle of something, so give me an hour?"

"Okay. See you then."

The line went silent. They'd never required a lot of words between them. He wanted to call Hannah so badly, but for once, he listened to his head, not his heart, and took a shower instead.

He was assaulted with thoughts of her in the bathroom, still a mess from caring for her the night before. The scent of her lingered in the room, and his clothes still lay in a damp pile on the floor. He scooped them all up and threw them in a clothes hamper in the closet.

He turned the water on and, without waiting for it to heat up, stepped in and washed away the sour coating this morning's events had left on his skin. After scrubbing his skin raw, he just stood under the shower head, letting the water run over him until he felt like a wet, pruney sponge.

He shut the water off, stepped out, dried off and walked to the closet to pull on some clothes. He was moving mechanically, no feeling, no emotion. All he wanted was to get out of this suite. Every room he walked into smelled like her. It had only been a half hour and he'd probably arrive at Ben's early, but he didn't care. He grabbed a jacket and his phone and took the elevator down to the lobby. He checked his phone on the way down to see if Hannah had called or texted, not that he expected she would have. There was nothing.

The valet brought his Jag around and he got in the car and sped off. Fifteen minutes later he pulled up in front of Ben's converted warehouse in SoHo. He was shocked to actually find a parking space less than a block from Ben's place as he pulled into it gratefully. He got out and was surprised to find Ben walking toward him.

As Ben approached, his eyes scanned Drew. "You look like shit."

He scoffed. "I feel like shit."

"Take it things didn't go well."

Drew stuffed his hands in his jacket pockets to warm them from the cold. "Things went to shit."

"Can you eat? I'm hungry as hell and there's a place around the corner I like."

Drew shrugged. "Whatever you want."

"It's this way." Ben walked past Drew and headed back in the direction his car had been parked. Ten minutes later they were walking through the doors of The Cupping Room. It was crowded, but it was obvious Ben was a regular when the waitress greeted him by name and gave him the first table that opened up. They sat down and two steaming cups of coffee were sitting in front of them in seconds.

"She doesn't want to see me again. I told her I loved her and she told me to fuck off." His soul resembled the liquid sitting in the cup in front of him. He cupped his hands around the mug. At least it didn't feel as cold as his heart right now.

Ben's good foot kicked him under the table.

"What the fuck?" He barked.

"A part of her life that she thought she had come to terms with just came crashing down around her. She's pissed." Ben stopped talking as a waitress came over to take their order. He ordered the special but Drew waved her off.

"I understand that, Ben, but none of it's my fault. She won't even try to figure something out."

"Listen, Drew, if there's one thing I know about, it's anger. Nothing you say to her right now is going to change how she's feeling. You're just going to have to give her some space to digest everything."

"And what do I do in the meantime?"

"You wait brother."

Drew ran a hand through his hair and blew out a breath. "This fucking sucks."

Hannah rinsed another dish and placed it in the strainer as she watched Grace and Emma play in her sister's backyard. Tammy brought another bowl in from the dining room and set it on the counter.

"I love having everyone over for Thanksgiving, but this part blows."

"What are you complaining about? I'm the one washing all these dishes."

Tammy grabbed a dish towel and started wiping. "But I did do all the cooking."

"But look at all the beautiful flowers I brought to decorate."

"Are you two arguing again?" They both turned their heads as Danny walked in and tore the towel out of Tammy's hand. "Go watch football with your husband. I'll do this."

"Okay, I won't argue with that." She stuck her tongue out at Hannah and giggled as she escaped the kitchen.

"You've been pretty quiet today. Everything okay?" He took a dish out of the strainer and picked up where Tammy had left off.

She hadn't seen much of her brother in the last month. She hadn't spoken to him about Drew, but Tammy had filled him in on some of the details. "Danny, can I ask you something about Jackson?"

"Of course, you know that. Anything." He came to a halt next to her.

"Did he talk to you about going back? After the accident? After the funerals?"

He shifted, leaning back against the counter, folding his arms at his chest. "We talked about a lot of things, but he didn't want to talk about that. I tried to get him to withdraw his request for another tour, but he told me he had already made the decision to go back before he had even come home. He did say that the accident only made it more clear that he was still needed over there."

The dish she was washing slipped from her fingers and fell with a clank into the soapy water. "What?"

"What?" His expression was one of confusion.

"What do you mean he decided to go back before? Before the accident?"

His head tilted. "Yeah. Didn't you know that?"

She threw her hands up in the air, soap suds flinging in different directions. "How would I know that? He barely spent any time with us when he was home then. He had promised me he was coming home after the last tour. I thought he signed back up because of the accident!"

He unfolded his arms and pulled her into an embrace. "Hannah, I'm sorry. I thought you knew that. I didn't realize."

She rested her head against his chest and blew out a tired breath. A thousand thoughts were running through her mind, but number one was that Ben wasn't the reason her husband had reenlisted. "I've made such a mess of things."

Her brother pushed her back and looked down at her. "What things? Why are you asking me about this now? It's been over two years."

She took the dish towel that was sitting on the counter and dried her hands before sitting at the kitchen table. "How come you've never mentioned Ben Sapphire to me?"

A frown appeared as sat beside her. "How do you know Ben?"

"Tammy told you about Drew?"

He nodded. "She told me you were dating a rich guy named Drew but that you had a falling out and to be extra nice to you today. That's about it."

She shook her head at her sister's overview of events. "His name is Drew Sapphire. Ben's brother."

He shrugged, still not connecting the dots. "Okay, and?"

She rolled her eyes in frustration. "Do you know how I figured out Ben knew Jackson?" She pointed at the area above her brother's heart. "The tattoo. He has it on his arm."

His eyes grew wide as he finally put things together. "Jesus, it really is a small world, isn't it?"

She shook her head and muttered, more to herself than to him, "You have no idea."

"But I don't understand what's wrong. Ben's a good guy. He was pretty messed up after the accident though."

"I know. His leg. All that. But how come you never told me about him? I mean, you obviously have a bond if you all share a tattoo together."

He looked down at his hands. "I don't know. A few reasons, I guess. Like I said, he was a mess after that accident. There was no way he could go to Jackson's funeral. When he heard what happened to Jackson, he tried to kill himself. He never said it was because of Jackson, but I think it was the last straw for him."

"Wait, he took that overdose because of Jackson?"

He cocked his head at her. "How'd you know it was an overdose?"

"Jesus, Danny. Are you listening? He is Drew's brother. Drew told me, but I thought it was before."

"I was the one who went to the hospital and told him about Jackson. He overdosed that night. Want to talk about feeling responsible?"

"Why didn't you tell me any of this? I should have known."

He spoke quietly then. "Hannah, you were a mess. When you disappeared after the funeral—" He reached out then and took one of her hands in his. "When we got you back, when you got home again, the last thing you needed was to deal with another soldier in pain. I wasn't going to do that to you."

Realization made her voice tremble. "Danny, I blamed him for Jackson. For everything. For going back. For his dying. For leaving us. I thought he was the one that told Jackson to go back. That he had talked him into reenlisting."

He squeezed her hand. "Then we'll go see him and you can talk to him."

She swallowed hard. "It's also the reason I told Drew I couldn't be with him. I said awful things to him. To both of them."

"Then you'll talk to both of them."

"What if he won't see me? What if I can't fix it?"

He shrugged, letting go of her hand. "There's only one way to find out."

Hannah eyed the big brick warehouse in SoHo as Danny turned into a parking lot across the street. "Must be nice to be neighbors with Justin Timberlake and Jay Z".

He raised an eyebrow. "Don't judge a book by its cover, Sis."

"What does that mean?" They were walking across the street toward the entrance of the building.

"You'll see." A knowing smile split his face. When they walked through the front door of the building, she paused to take everything in. The entire first floor of the warehouse had been converted into a gym and rehabilitation center. There were several men, and a few women, all disabled in some way scattered throughout the gym, working out. Some were being assisted by trainers, while others worked with each other. But what caught her eye and stilled her heart was the sign on the back wall.

BAKER-LANDON-ROSE MEMORIAL GYM

The names of the three men in Jackson's unit that had died.

"What is this?" she asked quietly.

"Ben started this about a year ago. Set up an entire gym with equipment disabled vets needed to get stronger. He hired specialized trainers and therapists who could work one on one with anyone who needs it. The membership has blown up in the last six months."

"This is amazing." She looked around at the people working out and marveled at the strength and determination she could see in many of their eyes.

"And that's not all. He doesn't charge any of them a dime. He also has mental health providers on staff with an open-door policy on the second floor. He wants to make sure he doesn't lose another soldier on his watch."

She had taken Ben at face value and had totally underestimated him. She continued looking around but stopped when her eyes locked with Ben's curious gaze. He leaned over and said something to the man he was working with before walking toward her. Her palms turned ice cold and sweaty as her heartbeat kicked up another notch.

His gaze slid from her to Danny, and Ben broke into a wide

grin. He slapped a hand on her brother's shoulder in greeting. "Danny Boy! This is a surprise."

"Hey, Little Boy Blue." They shook hands and then Danny turned toward her. "I brought someone to see you."

"I see that." Ben's gaze shifted to Hannah and he extended a tentative hand to greet her. "Hannah."

Instead of taking his hand, she lurched forward and wrapped her arms around him in a quick hug. An "Oh!" fell from his lips as she backed up just as quickly. She brought her hands together, fidgeting as she spoke. "Hello, Ben. Could we talk? Do you have a few minutes?"

"Sure. Let's go to my office." He turned to Danny. "You coming?"

"Nah. I'm going to hang out and say hi to a few folks."

She gave her brother's hand a quick squeeze. "Thanks, Danny."

She followed Ben's lead as he turned and walked through the gym, saying hello to some as he passed, until they reached a door on the other side. He held it open for her and closed it behind her again, then sat behind a desk in the room. She scanned the room quickly and noted the American flag that hung on the wall and the bookshelf that contained numerous framed pictures of him, Drew and fellow soldiers, books and several medals.

Her eyes stopped on a box on his desk containing a dozen loose black-stemmed roses. "You're the one that leaves the roses on Jackson's grave?"

His cheeks reddened as he looked at the roses and then back at her. "It's just my way of honoring them. I don't want them to think I've forgotten." He pointed to a chair next to the desk. "Sit down if you'd like."

She did before he could see that her knees were practically knocking together from nerves. "That's a nice thing to do. Really nice."

He just nodded curtly. "So, this is a surprise."

She cleared her throat. "I know. I'm sorry, I hope it's okay that I just showed up."

He stared at her a moment before responding. "What can I do for you?"

Her hands were in her lap, fingers fidgeting again. She met his wary gaze. "I came because I realized I owed you an apology about Jackson. "

She inhaled as if trying to drag in more courage and continued in a rush. "I know now that you didn't ask him to go back. I know it wasn't your fault. And I'm sorry. So sorry, Ben. Because I know what happened to him was just as hard for you as it was for me. I'm sorry I didn't listen to you. And I'm sorry for what I said to you. I was so wrong."

She hung her head then, afraid to look him in the eye. Afraid that he might tell her to go to hell. Afraid he wouldn't accept her apology. She heard his chair scrape back and she tensed, waiting for the inevitable order to leave.

A hand on her arm pulled her up and then into an embrace. "Thank you."

He hugged her tightly. After a moment of profound surprise, she wrapped her arms around him and hugged him back. He pulled away then and turned quickly, wiping at his cheeks before leaning against the desk. She looked at him with new eyes, taking in the man now, and not the enemy she had painted him to be. "I'm sorry too."

She shook her head in confusion. "What for?"

"I should have come to see you. After. Even if it was six months later, I should have." He looked down at the tattoo on his hand and then back up at her. "I guess I thought I was honoring him with this tattoo, and by visiting his grave, but I really should have honored him by going to see you. And his daughter. I should have made sure you were both okay."

"I guess we both could have done some things differently."

He told her then that's why he'd started this gym. He wanted returning vets, physically or mentally damaged, to have a place to come to and feel safe. Every one of them had served their country, and he understood what they had been through. He wanted to believe he was helping in some small way. He wanted to make up for not helping Jackson when he needed it.

"I understand what it's like to be in that dark place. I went there after Jackson died."

She touched his arm. "This is a really, really good thing you're doing. You're a good man."

He patted her hand and then pushed himself up off the desk. She stood then as well and was about to leave, but she couldn't without asking about Drew. "How is he?"

He grunted. "I was wondering if you were going to ask."

"I was afraid to, actually, but I need to know."

"Go see him. He hasn't left the hotel suite since you fought."

Her eyes opened in shock. "That was six days ago!"

"Yep. I tried to drag him out of there yesterday for Thanksgiving, but no go."

Her gut clenched in guilt. "Will he even see me?"

"Only one way to find out." This was starting to feel too familiar.

CHAPTER FOURTEEN

Drew hit mute on the stereo remote at the ding of the elevator arriving. The doors slid open with a whoosh. He stood up and slammed his glass of tequila down on the table. Goddamn it all to hell. He had told Ben yesterday to just leave him alone.

He stormed out of the living room and skidded to a halt when his eyes landed on the shadowed form in his foyer. "Hannah? Is that you?"

Her voice cut through the darkened room like a beacon. "Why are all the lights off?"

"I like it like this." His tone wasn't kind. "What are you doing here?"

Her footsteps sounded and then the click of a switch being flipped. Bright light flooded the foyer and he raised his hand to cover his squinting eyes. He heard the sharp intake of a breath and then her hand was on his shoulder. He flinched.

"Drew, how long has it been since you've eaten or showered?" Her voice was soft and maternal.

His eyes were adjusting to the light so he lowered his hand, blinking rapidly, as if waking up from a bad dream.

"Are you really here?" He reached out to touch her and was

surprised when he actually made contact. He stroked her hair, taking a lock in his hand and smelling it. He gave her a sloppy smile. "You always smell so good."

She gently pulled the hair from his hand, and a small smile graced her face without quite reaching her eyes. "Are you drunk?"

"Am I drunk?" He threw his hands up and laughed maniacally. "Not enough if I can still see you."

"Oh, Drew."

He swayed slightly as she dropped her purse on the floor and then her coat on top of it. She took his hand. "Come with me, okay?"

He liked when her voice was soft like this. He let her lead him through his bedroom and into the bathroom. She turned lights on as she went, then let go of his hand and pulled a stool up to the sink. She grabbed a bottle of shampoo out of the shower.

"Come sit over here." She pointed to the stool, and because he didn't know what else to do, he went. Behind him, water started to flow. Her hands were at his waist and then his shirt was being pulled up. "Lift your arms up, Drew."

He lifted and she pulled the shirt up over his head and dropped it on the floor. She took a towel then and wrapped it around his shoulders, brushing her hand over the thick scruff that layered his face. "Let's get you cleaned up, okay?"

She laid her hand flat on his chest and pushed him back. Her hand moved to his head and her fingers ran through his hair, pulling his head back gently. She scooped water from the faucet and he sighed when the warm liquid made contact with his head. He closed his eyes and let himself relax as her fingers continued to weave through his hair.

He smelled the shampoo before its coolness hit his scalp, and then her fingers were massaging his head. He let out a contented sigh.

"Does that feel good?" Her warm breath at his ear made goose bumps break out across his chest and arms. More warm water spilled over his head as she rinsed the soap from his hair. The water shut off and the towel around his shoulders was pulled free and settled over his head. He closed his eyes and enjoyed being in the darkness again for a moment.

The towel slid out of his hair and was draped back around his shoulders again. He blinked his eyes open. She stood next to him, eyes on his face. "Can I shave you?"

He didn't have the strength or will to do it. He closed his eyes again. "Okay."

She pulled open a drawer and he heard foam coming from a can and then felt the cool cream as she spread it over his face. Her touch was light and gentle and made him want to kiss her. He opened his eyes and watched her movements as she worked. She locked eyes with his and her hand stilled.

"Okay?"

He just nodded and looked away. He heard the water turn on again and then she was standing over him with his razor in hand.

"Up or down?"

"Up my neck, down my face."

The razor touched the bottom of his throat and then scraped up and through the stubble. When she reached his chin, she rinsed the razor and began again. He shut his eyes and lay still as the razor rasped against his throat.

Ten minutes later, a hot wash cloth was rinsing his face, and then her cool hand was trailing lightly over his smooth skin.

He sat up then, opening his eyes, and caught her wrist in his hand. She met his eyes and pulled her wrist out of his grasp. "Better."

She turned, walked to the shower, opened the door and started the water. When she seemed satisfied with the temperature, she walked to the closet and took out another towel. "Take a shower. I'm going to make you something to eat."

Not giving him time to digest her order or refuse, she left the bathroom and shut the door behind her. He sat on the stool and tried to remember what day it was. He'd lost track between tequila shots. Was it yesterday that Ben was here? His head was foggy and he couldn't remember the last time he'd eaten or slept.

How many days had he been sitting here, waiting for her to come to him? And now she was here and he didn't know what to say, what to do.

The door opened suddenly. Her body leaned halfway through the opening. "Drew. Get. In. The. Shower." The door banged shut.

Fifteen minutes later, in a fresh pair of sweats and a clean T-shirt, he left his room and walked into the kitchen. His stomach clenched and grumbled loudly as the smell of bacon assaulted him. She had made toast and scrambled eggs and had fresh juice all sitting on the table. She was setting a plate of bacon down on the table when she spotted him.

She smiled and his heart stuttered. Just seeing her here, even if he didn't know what it meant yet, made his heart beat a little less painfully than an hour ago. She motioned for him to sit down. "Come eat. You look like you've lost ten pounds."

He looked down at himself, frowning, and then shuffled to the table. He picked up the fork and started eating. He was three bites in when he realized he was starving and began wolfing it down. Her hand landed on his forearm, and he froze.

"Hey, slow down. I don't want you to get sick."

He grunted, but did as she requested and started chewing his food instead of inhaling it. After several minutes, he put down his fork and picked up the orange juice, draining it in a few gulps. He stood and walked over to where Hannah was standing.

"Why are you here?" He wasn't angry anymore. Instead, he was confused. The tequila was wearing off and he was starting to slip back into reality.

"I came to talk to you, but when I got here, and when I saw you—" She lowered her voice. "I needed to make sure you were all right first."

He scoffed. "You think I'm okay now?"

She shook her head. "No. I just mean . . . Drew, you looked so . . . so broken."

He barely spoke above a whisper. "Hannah, I am broken. And I'm tired. So fucking tired."

He stepped back, turned and starting walking to the bedroom. "I can't do this again. Please, just leave." He didn't look back. He didn't want to see her face. He didn't want to hear anything else. He didn't want to fight anymore. He shut the door, shut off all the lights, climbed into bed and let the darkness claim him.

"Hannah?" A hand gently swept hair off of her face as her eyes flickered open. Drew's smooth face was inches from hers, his blue eyes filled with concern. She sat up quickly as she remembered where she was.

"What are you doing here?" His voice was no longer angry or accusatory, just curious.

She rubbed the sleep out of her eyes before meeting his nervously. "Don't you remember last night?"

His hand ran through his hair and a small smile touched his lips. "I remember you washing my hair. That felt nice."

She returned his smile with a small one of her own. "You were a bit of a mess. I didn't know what else to do. You were a little bit drunk."

He sat on the couch next to her. "Tequila and I have been really good friends again."

"I'm sorry, Drew." The apology fell from her lips before she had time to think. "I came to tell you that last night and then when I found you." She shrugged before continuing. "You were just so sad. I had to do something. So, I washed your hair, and shaved you, and fed you."

His hand scrubbed down his face in memory as she described what she had done the night before. "And I couldn't leave again. Not until I had a chance to at least tell you I was sorry."

Her pulse was thrumming wildly and she was talking way too

fast but she was afraid he was going to tell her to leave again and she just wanted to say what she needed to say before he did.

He didn't though. He just stared at her, his eyes pensive, as if he couldn't be sure he'd heard her correctly. "You're sorry?"

She scooted closer and touched his knee, needing contact. "I'm so sorry. Sorry I said the things I said to you. Sorry I didn't stop and listen to your brother. Sorry I didn't trust that we could have figured this out. I'm sorry for so many things, but when I saw you last night—" Out of air, she took a hasty breath. "When I saw what I did to you. My heart broke into a thousand pieces for the hurt I put you through."

A small frown appeared on his face. "I don't understand. Don't get me wrong, my heart leapt out of my chest when I walked in here and saw you sleeping on my couch. All I wanted to do was lie down beside you and pull you into my arms because I've missed you so fucking much. But, what's changed in a week?"

Her heart sank at the doubt in his voice. Was she too late? Had he already closed his heart to her? "Everything's changed. Everything."

She shifted even closer and this time took one of his hands into her own. He tensed at first, but then relaxed as she wrapped both her hands around it tightly. "I talked to my brother, and to yours."

His eyebrows flew up in surprise. "You saw Benny?"

"Yesterday. But let me tell you why. I talked to my brother about what happened with us and why, and he told me that Jackson had reenlisted before the accident even happened. He had always planned to go back."

She shook her head angrily but rambled on as different emotions played across Drew's face. "I was so wrong about everything. About my husband and why he did what he did. About your brother. And for how I treated you because of it all. I should have had more faith in you. In us. And I didn't. Instead, I ran away and hid in my anger again."

She hung her head, trying to hide her shame and embarrassment, but also because she was afraid of what his face might reveal.

"I realize now that no one but Jackson made that decision to go back. Even if Ben had asked him to go back, it was still Jackson. He made that choice. The choice to leave us. I just wanted— No, I needed someone to blame."

His hand slid out from between hers and any hope she had for reconciliation went with it. She whimpered. His hand was under her chin then, lifting it up so that her face was even with his. He was inches from her. "Don't ever run away on me again. Ever."

Her heart lurched in her chest as hope flowed in again. She shook her head frantically. "I won't. Ever. I promise."

"I want to know everything, Hannah. I do." His hand shifted from her chin to her cheek. "But right now, all I want to do is hold you. I've missed you so goddamn much."

He moved then and brought his lips to hers in the softest of kisses. His lips sealed tenderly over hers, his actions slow and deliberate as he seemed to taste every area of her mouth. When he broke away from her, he slid his arms around her and held her tightly. He just held her and so she wrapped her arms around him tightly and held him back, so grateful for his forgiveness and to feel him again. His breath was hot on her ear as he whispered, "I missed you. So much."

She shifted then and straddled his waist. He cradled her face and began peppering kisses everywhere on her face but her lips. When he had covered every inch of her face, he moved down her neck, pulling her collar aside to expose her shoulder.

His tongue grazed over the light mark of his love bite, and then he pulled her shirt over her head. Before it even hit the floor, Hannah began tugging his off as well. No words were spoken. They moved in sync, desperate to feel each other again.

As soon as his shirt was gone, she leaned forward and relished the feeling of his bare skin against hers. His soft chest hair tickled the sensitive buds of her breasts into hard points. Their lips were fused together, their breaths becoming one, as she rocked her core slowly up and down the hard length of him. He broke away from their kiss and wrapped her hair in his fist, pulling her head back, and rained kisses down her neck, her clavicle and finally her breasts. He pulled one into his mouth and swirled his tongue around the elongated nipple before suckling.

Hannah pushed herself deeper into his mouth, lost in the slow rising heat he was bringing to her surface. He let go of her nipple, kissed his way across her chest and slid the other one into his mouth. She might combust just from the sensations he sent coursing through her. This was so slow and gentle and it meant so much more than the other times they'd had sex.

She pushed herself up and off Drew and started sliding her jeans down and off her legs. She pointed to Drew's sweats. "Off. Now."

He chuckled. "Always so anxious. I love that about you."

He quickly untied the string on the sweats and, raising his hips, slid the material down over his waist and off his legs. His cock sprang up, hard and ready.

"Don't you ever wear underwear?"

"Easier access. Come back here."

He didn't have to order her twice as she slid atop him again. She didn't have the patience or restraint to wait another second and positioned herself over his cock, guiding it inside as she lowered herself down. They both moaned in unison, her head falling back, before Drew's hand reached around her neck and pulled her to his lips. In between kisses, he breathed out a command: "Move."

Hannah began rocking her pelvis back and forth, sliding her pussy up and down his cock, leaving it wet and throbbing. With each forward motion, her clit rubbed up against the base of his shaft and pulsed in response. "Oh my god. You always feel so good."

Drew latched onto one of her peaked nipples, sucking hard, biting the tip gently. Her hips surged harder against him, and her clit began to tighten.

"Drew, I'm going to come." Hannah's hips plunged quickly now, increasing the pressure of her clit against his cock, her breath leaving her in small gasps.

"Come, Hannah. I want to feel all of you."

His permission was all it took for her orgasm to detonate. She clenched her eyes as her muscles clenched onto Drew's cock, sparks of light bursting behind her lids, a mewl of relief leaving her mouth. He clamped his mouth over hers with a growl, clutching her, as his release spurted into her.

Her clit pulsed around his cock for a few more beats before both of their bodies relaxed. She lifted her head off his shoulder and brought her forehead against his, their eyes locking on one another. He leaned in and kissed her slowly, then pulled away, meeting her eyes again.

"I love you, Hannah. I wasn't sure how you felt and I didn't want to push you. But I do. I love you."

Her breath caught at his words, but instead of being scared, she was relieved. She had been so worried he wouldn't take another chance on her, and it took almost losing him to make her realize she had fallen in love with him too. Before she could respond, he started talking quickly again.

"I know it's too soon. I know it's too fast. I know we've both made mistakes. But every single minute of every single day, all I want is to have you next to me. When you aren't here, I just feel empty."

She was struck speechless by his words so she simply nodded. Drew moved his hands up and gripped her lightly around each arm, breaking her hold from around his neck, pushing her further back.

"Can you say something? Please?" His voice was laced with concern and worry.

"I think I love you too," she whispered. She was surprised to realize it was true.

A smile broke out across his face as he pulled her back into an embrace. Then he pulled away again. "Wait, you think?"

"I just— This is— I never thought I would be here again."

"I never thought I'd be here again either. Ever. But here we are."

She let out a shaky laugh. "Yes, here we are. And I'm terrified."

He pulled her into his lap, his arms holding her close. "Of what?"

"Of everything. Of loving you. Of losing you. Of what this means. We lead such different lives. I have a child. I thought I had my life all figured out and then, you."

"It's as simple or as hard as we make it. We'll figure it all out. We have to."

"We have to?" She couldn't keep the question out of her voice.

He smiled wistfully. "Yes, we have to. I love you, Hannah Rose, and I'm not letting you go now that I have you."

"What about Grace?"

He looked at her in confusion. "What about Grace? She's a part of you. I'll love her as much as I love you."

"Just like that?"

"Just like that. People fall in love with single parents all the time."

"But you live so richly. I live in an apartment over a flower shop I barely can call my own. How does all this work?"

He shrugged. "I don't know yet. But we don't have to figure it all out today. Let's just be us for a little while."

"But—"

Drew placed a finger on her lips. "No more questions. Stop overthinking it. I only have one more question for you."

"Okay?" she mumbled around his finger. He lifted it again. "Do you love me?" His soft voice was laced with fear.

She brought her eyes up to his and nodded. "Yes, I do."

A wide grin broke across his face. "Say it."

She smiled back at him and then sat up straighter. "I love you. I love you, Andrew Sapphire."

He pulled her face to his and crushed his lips against hers, kissing her hungrily. "I love you too."

CHAPTER FIFTEEN

Hannah pulled her jacket around herself tightly and tugged her scarf higher over her face. It was a cold, raw January day and the wind was unforgiving. She stood in the snow over Jackson's grave, a man standing next to her. He was using his cane today so he wouldn't slip in the snow.

He bent at the waist to lay a bouquet of black roses against the white marble. His hand rested against the top of the stone as he bent back up, his lips moving silently for a few minutes. He looked at her then and shrugged. "I wanted him to know I'll always look out for you."

She grasped his hand and squeezed it, not letting go. "Thank you, Benjamin."

A lot had happened in the two months since she had discovered that Drew's brother and her husband had served together in Iraq. Most important was the peace she had seemed to make with herself and with Ben over Jackson's death.

Now, with her hand in the crook of his elbow as they walked across the snowy graveyard back to his car, she only felt love and respect for him. The anger was gone. When they reached his car, he opened the passenger door for her and helped her inside.

They were headed back to the city to meet with Drew and Grace.

"You okay?" He looked over at her.

"Yep." She glanced over at him. "You?"

"Yep." He smiled at her. "Excited about tonight?"

"Nervous. I hope your parents will be happy about everything."

He grinned. "Trust me, Hannah, they are going to be thrilled."

D rew had Grace wrapped up in one of his arms, her little arms around his neck, while his other hand held Hannah's as they entered his parents' house. "Mom? Dad? We're here."

His mother appeared gracefully from another room and greeted them all with hugs and kisses. "Hannah, how nice to see you again. And Grace, you too."

They had begun joining his parents for their weekly family dinners shortly after he and Hannah had reconciled.

His mother wrapped her hands around his middle when he reached down to hug her, patting her hands on his back. "How's my baby boy?"

He rolled his eyes and placed a kiss on her cheek. "Mom, I'm not your baby anymore."

"Oh, you'll always be my baby." She patted him on the arm and then turned and motioned for them to follow her through the foyer to the dining room. "Come, dinner is all set. Ben is already at the table with your father."

When they entered the room, his father stood up and met him with a half-hug and a slap to the shoulder. "Andrew."

His father's face lit up at the sight of Gracie. It always amazed him how such a little girl could wrap a grown man around her finger so easily. She was a living reminder to his parents of what it was to have a little girl in the house again. They had loved his little sister fiercely, and having Grace here had brought them back to life.

His father scooped Grace out of his arms and gave her a big hug and kiss. "How's my favorite girl?"

She giggled and clutched his face in her two little hands and kissed him on the nose. His father's face turned a light pink, and his smile turned even brighter. Yep, Dad is a goner.

"Hi, Mr. Sapphire."

His father lowered Grace to the floor and then reached over to kiss Hannah on the cheek. "And my other favorite girl? How are you?"

Hannah brushed a kiss back on his cheek and smiled warmly at him. "We're good."

"Okay, let's sit down and eat then. I'm starving. Grace, come sit next to me."

Drew shook his head and smiled to see his father in this light. He hadn't been this happy and relaxed in a long time. They all took a seat and began passing food around the table, chatting and eating casually. After dinner, his mother brought out bowls of ice cream topped with whipped cream for everyone.

It was then that Drew decided to share their news. He reached over and took Hannah's hand, squeezing it before placing it in his lap. She smiled knowingly at him. He cleared his throat and tapped his spoon against his bowl to get everyone's attention.

"So, as much as we love coming to have dinner once a week with you now, Hannah and I actually wanted to meet with you tonight to share some news with you."

He looked over at Hannah again, smiling warmly, and then stood up. "As you know by now, when I met Hannah, she sent me into a tailspin and stole my heart in one fell swoop. We haven't been together very long, but neither of us wants to wait another second to spend our life together, so I'm happy to share with all of you that Hannah has agreed to marry me."

He pulled her up then and kissed her passionately on the lips. They were met with cheers of joy and congratulations from around the table. When he pulled apart from her, his mother was at their side and pulling Hannah's left hand up to look at her empty ring finger.

"No ring?" She turned and looked at Drew in question.

"Not yet, Mom." He took Hannah's hand and brought it to his lips in a kiss.

"I just finally got her to say yes last night. But don't worry, it's coming."

H annah walked off the elevator into Drew's suite and let out a gasp of surprise at what she saw. Lit candles were on every surface, bathing everything in soft twinkling light. Van Morrison played softly from somewhere further in the suite, and the scent of roses was everywhere. At her feet, soft white petals were scattered in a path leading her inside the apartment.

She ambled down the trail of petals, taking in every detail of the room as she went, until she was standing in the middle of the living room. Drew had said he wanted to take her to dinner, so she was wearing a burgundy dress with the black heels he had given to her on their first "official" date. She looked around the room and marveled at the number of candles that were lit and the bouquets of white roses that filled every available space.

She flinched in surprise as Drew's hands slid around her waist and then pulled him against her in a hug. "Hello, princess. You look beautiful."

She spun and wrapped her arms around his neck, then pulled herself up to his lips for a kiss. Breathless, she broke free. "Drew, what is this? It's amazing."

He dropped another kiss against her mouth. "Do you like it?"

"Yes, it's absolutely breathtaking."

He nodded and began swaying with her to the music. "Do you remember this song?"

She bit her lip as she remembered the dance they had shared

the first time she went to his house in the Hamptons. And then blushed when she remembered how they'd made love afterward. It was the first time she'd admitted to herself that she was falling in love with him. "Of course I remember."

"I remember too. I remember how beautiful your hair looked as loose strands blew in the wind when we walked on the beach. And I remember how happy you were eating leftovers from my fridge. And how your face lit up when you laughed while we danced. But mostly I remember making love to you and knowing in that moment that you were the woman I wanted to spend the rest of my life with."

He let go of her then and knelt down in front of her, taking her left hand in his. Her other hand rose to her mouth, trying to cover the smile that broke out across her face. He slid a ring out of his pocket and held it in his other hand.

"Hannah Marie Rose, I love you more than I could have ever thought possible. You are the very breath that makes my heart beat. You are the sunshine that warms me. You are everything that makes my world whole. Will you please do me the honor of becoming my wife?"

Tears of joy streamed down her face as she nodded and jumped up and down and then into his arms. He wrapped his arms around her tightly and spun her around the room before putting her down and kissing away her tears. She was laughing and crying and trying to kiss him all at the same time.

She'd never ever thought her heart could feel this full again. He pulled away for a second, lifted her hand to slide the ring onto her finger. It was a beautiful princess-cut diamond, completely surrounded by smaller diamonds and set in a diamond-encrusted band. She looked at it on her finger and then crushed her lips to Drew's again.

"It's absolutely beautiful."

"Is that a yes?" She realized then that she hadn't even given him an answer. She grinned so broadly her cheeks hurt. "Yes, Drew. Of course, I'll marry you!"

He cupped her face in his hands then and kissed her lips gently.

"I love you, Drew."

"I love you more."

EPILOGUE

Hannah waddled to the side of the bed and shook Drew awake. "It's time."

Drew sat bolt upright in the bed and looked at her in wild-eyed panic. "It's time?"

"It's time. My water broke an hour ago."

He jumped out of bed and started running around, pulling clothes on erratically. "What do you mean an hour ago? Why did you wait so long to wake me?"

Hannah laughed under her breath as her husband struggled into his pants. "The baby isn't going to drop out of me, Drew. It could take hours. I have done this before, remember?"

"Oh shit. Where's Grace?"

She shook her head, kind of enjoying the sight of him completely falling apart. "Tammy came and got her. That's why I waited to wake you up." She waddled out of the bedroom. "I'll be waiting in the kitchen when you're ready."

She shook her head as he swore in frustration while hunting for his shoes. Men. As she sat in the kitchen, she looked around and smiled at the wonderful home she and Drew had made together. They had flown to St. John one month after he'd proposed and were married on a beautiful, white sandy beach. It was exactly how they both wanted it. Simple and just the three of them. Grace was delighted to act as flower girl and maid of honor. They had both already been married before and didn't want to make a fuss over a big ceremony. They just wanted to be married and to start their life together.

Just last week, she turned the keys of the shop over to Robin to run for her while she navigated having and raising baby number two. She'd be there to help as needed, and would most likely go back again once they'd all gotten into a new routine, but she was thrilled to give Robin this opportunity. Making things even easier was Robin's decision to move into her apartment when she and Drew had moved in together.

They still had the house in the Hamptons, but Drew no longer spent nights in his hotel suite. They'd bought a loft several buildings down from Ben and had it renovated into a home they could grow into. Four bedrooms, five baths, a huge kitchen and living space for them all. The city was their playground. Grace was in first grade now and attended a private school that Hannah brought her to daily.

They saw Ben almost every day and were surprised if Drew's dad didn't stop in any less than three times a week. Gracie had her uncle and grandfather wrapped around her little finger and had become the apple of their eyes. Yes, life was so much better than she could have ever imagined or hoped for.

Drew stumbled out from their bedroom, her hospital bag in hand, his hair in a thousand different directions. God, she loved this man.

"You ready there, Superman?"

He looked up and grinned at her. "I know, I'm a fucking mess. But Jesus, woman, you're having my damn baby today."

She looked down, rubbed her belly and winced in pain as a contraction hit her.

He ran over to her and took her hand. "Breathe, honey, just breathe."

She swatted him away. "Are you kidding me?"

The contraction passed and she stood up straight again. "Okay, let's go have a baby."

———————

E ighteen hours later, Grace stroked the dark, downy locks on her baby brother and then, frowning, looked over at Hannah lying in her hospital bed. "I think Brody is a weird name, Mom."

She chuckled and then raised her eyebrows in surprise. "What's so weird about it? Brody was my dad's name."

"Mom, it rhymes with grody. Do you know how many kids will pick on him when he gets older?" Grace was shaking her head back and forth as if this should be so obvious.

She laughed again. "Well, I can't change it now. You'll just have to make sure that no one picks on him. That's what big sisters are for."

A knock came at the door then, interrupting any further discussion on the subject. Grace jumped off the bed and over to the door to open it. "Grandma and Grandpa are finally here!"

Caroline and Gavin strode into the room, arms filled with flowers, balloons and a big, blue teddy bear, wide smiles on their faces. Caroline deposited her contents on the closest surface and walked quickly to Hannah, small tears of joy leaking from the corners of her eyes.

"Let me see my grandson!" She bent down and dropped a quick kiss on Hannah's forehead before leaning down further to place a softer kiss on Brody's head. "Can I hold him?"

"Of course!" Hannah lifted her son up toward her mother-in-law. "Meet your grandson, Brody James Sapphire."

Gavin had moved closer and was standing next to Caroline, and as she took the baby into her arms, he reached out and swept a gentle caress over the baby's head. "He's absolutely beautiful, Hannah. He looks just like Andrew did when he was a baby."

"Speaking of Drew, he should be back anytime. He went home to shower and change." Hannah looked up at the clock on the wall, noting that he had been gone a little over two hours. She was just about to grab her phone to text him when the door swung open again, and Ben and Drew walked in. Her face lit up to see her husband. He still made her heart race. "Look who I found out in the hallway."

Ben clasped Drew's shoulder as a wide grin broke across his face. "My baby brother is a dad!"

Drew walked over to the bed and sat down next to Hannah before kissing her softly on the lips. "Hey, gorgeous. How are you?"

"Happy that you're back."

"Do you need anything?"

"Nope." She looked around the room at the people she loved and was filled with a sense of absolute happiness, gratitude and peace. She smiled back up at him. "I'm perfect."

Author Note:

Thanks so much for reading the conclusion of The Auction Series! Drew and Hannah are my very first book couple, and mean more to me than any of my other characters. If you'd like to read more about the Sapphires, check out my book, Breaking Benjamin. It's all about Ben, aka Benny, and his attempt to snag 'the one'. It's a stand-alone and can be purchased here from any retailer:
books2read.com/u/bW9Zo1

There's a sneak peek of the first chapter in just a few more pages, so keep reading to check it out!

Word-of-mouth is crucial to any author. If you enjoyed this book, it would be so appreciated if you left a review online. It only needs to be one or two sentences, but it makes all the difference in the world. Thank you so much.

xoxo Michelle

Amazon Review link: https://goo.gl/3tH1of

BookBub Review link: https://goo.gl/TGCrbN

ACKNOWLEDGMENTS

First, always first, a huge thank you to my husband Doug, who not only has always encouraged me to follow my dreams, but also helps me chase them. I couldn't do any of this without him, and I thank my lucky stars that I ended up with him. I love you more... no matter what you say.

My boys; Tyler and Tommy, my young men now. The absolute truest loves of my life. Thank you for all the patience you have when I'm in writer mode, for always supporting me, and for not complaining too much about all the take-out. I'm sure Brother's Pizza isn't complaining either...

A special thanks to my personal assistant, my super squirrel, Amanda Walker. You somehow manage to put up with all my silly, crazy, blonde, un-photoshopping ways to make sure everything that needs to get done, gets done. One can only wonder what my pages would look like without you. #NerdsRule

I've been really blessed to have a few blogs and bloggers support me and my work unconditionally. Bloggers are a special breed— they do what they do for the love of stories and generally make no money at all. While there have been many blogs and readers that have supported me, all with my extreme thanks, this group of girls have gone above and beyond the call of duty. They will always have a special place in my heart. In no particular order, my sincere gratitude goes to the following:

Gina Morgan at The Three Bookateers
Nikki Pearce at Jacqueline and Nikki's Book Corner
Karrie Puskas at Panty Dropping Book Blog
Dusty Summerford at Reviews by Red
Donna Wolz at Wise Owl's PR
Tiffany Burnett-Busbey at Book Relations

To my beautiful daughter Felicia and my friend Connie, thank you for the amazing swag you both create for me. The pretties you make add so much brightness and sparkle to my little book world!

And last, but not least, to my family and friends for your continued love and support. You know who you are. Xoxo

ABOUT THE AUTHOR

Michelle Windsor is a wife, mom, and a writer who lives North of Boston with her family. When she isn't spinning stories, she's been known to partake in good wine and good food with her family and friends. She's a voracious reader, loves to hike with her German shepherd, Roman, enjoys a good romance movie and may be slightly obsessed with Outlander.

You can find Michelle on her webpage at www.authormichellewindsor.com , on Facebook at www.facebook.com/authormwindsor or on Instagram at https://www.instagram.com/author_michelle_windsor/.

If you'd like to keep up to date with all things Michelle Windsor, including upcoming releases, you can subscribe to her newsletter here: http://eepurl.com/ciizN1 Each new subscriber is sent a free copy of her book, Losing Hope.

ALSO BY MICHELLE WINDSOR

The Winning Bid:
Universal Link: http://books2read.com/u/mey2KZ

Losing Hope:
Universal Link: books2read.com/u/brYoyY

Love Notes:
Universal Link: books2read.com/u/mYrgxo

Tempting Secrets:
Universal Link: books2read.com/u/49WPLY

Tempting Tricks:
Universal Link: books2read.com/u/4XRo29

Breaking Benjamin:
Universal Link: books2read.com/u/bW9Zo1

Marrying Benjamin:
Universal Link: books2read.com/u/bMZrNXBook 3

SNEAK PEEK

I shove two fingers between my collar and neck and tug hard as I stride through the revolving door of our newest hotel. This damn tie is strangling me. It's bad enough I have to make an appearance at these events, but Drew's insistence that I wear a suit and tie is pure torture for me and he knows it.

Fuck it. I grasp the knot of the tie, loosen it, and yank the noose-like silk over my head, shoving the offending article in my jacket pocket. I unbutton the top two buttons of my shirt as well, letting out a sigh of pleasure at the ability to breathe freely again. What's Drew going to do, fire me? He can't. I own thirty percent of the company, just like him.

Just to really get under his skin, I stop at the coat check, swap my suit jacket for a ticket, and grin widely. I thank the attendant who has just unwittingly helped me to drag at least one eye roll out of my younger brother this evening. Yep, Drew is my younger brother, but he does more to keep me on the straight and narrow than the other way around.

After spending seven years in the Army, three of those years deployed overseas for active duty, he understands that my edges will always be a little rough. But that doesn't stop him from trying to smooth them out when he can.

Strolling into the grand ballroom, I smile as a swell of pride courses through me. The latest hotel in our chain, Sapphire Resorts, has turned out beautifully, and without a doubt, I believe it's going to be a big success, especially with the location so central to the financial district. *When did I start caring so much about this shit?* I chuckle softly with a small shake of my head and then look for the closest bar. I need a drink if I'm going to get through the next two hours.

I head to the back corner of the ballroom, a spot I know will most likely be a bit quieter, but pause when a flash of gold catches the corner of my eye. I turn my head and draw in a long, appreciative breath as I scan the beauty making her way across the room. Her gaze seems focused on the bar at the front of the room, so I turn my body and casually drift in that direction instead.

As I'm walking, I scan from her gold-clad toes, up her bare, toned legs to mid-thigh, where the hem of her sheer cream dress ends. The sheer fabric is scattered with a thousand different types of golden gemstones that hug her tiny waist and perfect breasts, reflecting against every light in the room.

But what really draws my attention is the open back of the dress. Her entire back is bare, exposing skin so smooth, it appears flawless. I clasp and unclasp my hand as I fight the urge to press it flat against her skin as I move closer. It's hard to tell if her hair is long or short because it's all piled on top of her head, as if she knows the power her exposed back possesses.

I stop several feet from the bar and watch as she attempts to cut a path through the mingling throng, waving to try to catch the bartender's attention. The bartender is female; otherwise, I'm certain she would have had a drink in front her before she lifted a single finger. I continue watching until a rather stout gentleman slides up beside her and attempts to make conversation. It's amusing to watch her try to be kind to the man until I see him reach out and slide his pinky finger down her arm suggestively, a look of disgust crossing her face at the action.

Anger surges through my body, and within seconds, I'm pushing myself between her and the man. A warning snarl slips from my lips as I glare at him, placing my hand flat against the center of her back. It feels like silk. It's the single thought that flies through my head before I smile down at her and brush a kiss against her cheek.

"Hello, darling. Are you having a problem getting the cocktails?"

Her wide blue eyes look up at me in surprise and then in knowing relief as she immediately plays into my little game. "Yes! Have you come to rescue me, babe?"

I can't help the wide grin that breaks across my face when she gives me a small wink and mouths silently, "Thank you so much".

"I have." I give her my full attention for only a second, my eyes locking onto hers long enough to see light grey flecks mixed into the blue surrounding her pupil, reminding me of waves churning at sea.

I break contact and look at the bartender's name tag. "Excuse me, Greta?" Whether it's because I'm a somewhat handsome male, or because she realizes a Sapphire is standing in front of her, suddenly, all of her attention is focused on me.

"Yes, sir, what can I get you?" Her cheeks turn a light pink as she fidgets with the bottle opener in her fingers.

I smile warmly to try to settle her nerves, nodding toward the back of the bar. "I'll have a couple fingers of that whiskey, please, on the rocks." I turn my head toward the vision in gold, locking my eyes with hers again. "And, darling, I'm sorry, what did you want again?"

I watch as her eyes narrow and one side of her gloss-lined lips tilt up in a smirk as she tells the bartender that she'll have a Goose on the rocks, her eyes never leaving mine.

Greta sets our drinks down in front of us within seconds, then busies herself with the next person in line. I watch as her delicate fingers, tipped with nails painted black, wrap around the glass and raise it to her mouth, her lips kissing the edge as she draws in a small sip of the clear liquid before slowly lowering it. "Thanks for rescuing me."

I look down in shock as the hand that was on her back is suddenly cold and empty. I watch her turn and walk away for only a second before I grab my whiskey off the bar and quickly follow, calling after her. "I'm Ben, in case you were wondering."

She stops mid-stride, anchors her foot and then spins around, stopping in front of me, a cocky grin on her face. "I wasn't. Wondering. But nice to meet you, Ben. Thanks again." She raises the glass in salute and moves to turn again, but I take a step closer as she does, causing her to falter, one eyebrow raising in curiosity. "Yes?"

"You aren't going to tell me your name?" *Jesus, I sound like a desperate idiot who's never seen a beautiful woman before.*

She laughs lightly and takes another sip from her glass, her eyes scanning me from head to toe then pausing briefly at what I'm sure are my tattoos peeking out of my open collar, and then shakes her head. "No, I don't think so."

I rear back in surprise and scoff. "You seriously aren't going to tell me your name?"

She shrugs and challenges me. "Why?"

"Why do I want to know your name?" My brows rise.

She nods and places a hand on her hip, jutting it out slightly as she does. "Yes, why? Are you planning on sending me flowers or are you just trying to get to know me better?" She lifts her glass a little in the air. "Do I owe you because you bought me a drink?"

A little unsure and a lot stunned by her response, I scratch my beard and frown down at her. "You're a spunky little thing, aren't you?"

She lifts her shoulders nonchalantly. "Maybe. Maybe I just know guys like you."

I raise my brows in surprise. "Guys like me?"

She nods and takes her hand off her hip to wave it up and down with a flourish around me. "Yes, guys like you: tall, dark and handsome." She gives me another once over before continuing. "And I'd say rich based on your watch and shoes alone."

I give her my most dazzling smile. "You think I'm handsome?"

A small frown tugs her lips down. "See? That's all you heard. Guys like you think they can throw their pretty little smiles around and we women are just supposed to fall at your feet."

"I wasn't expecting you to fall at my feet. I was just wondering what your name is."

She lifts the glass to her lips again, the ice clinking as she drains the rest of the vodka, and then takes a step closer to hand me the glass. "Like I said, thanks for the drink." She looks me up and down one final time, shakes her head, and then mutters as she turns to leave, "Been there, done that. Not going there again."

Dumbfounded, I watch her walk back through the crowd, her beautiful bare back taunting me as she does. I raise my own glass in response, finishing the whiskey in one swallow. As I lower the glass, I notice Gage, my friend and photographer we hired for the evening, taking some pictures at the edge of the room. I quickly walk back to the bar, deposit the empty glasses, and ask Greta for two beers. Grabbing them, I relocate Gage and make my way over to him.

"Hey, man! How's it going?" I hold one of the beers out to him, which he takes, a grateful look on his face.

"Thanks, man. I need this." He takes a long pull from the bottle. "The shoot is going great. I'm just about done I think. Just want to get some of your brother's speech and then I think I can wrap up."

"Thanks again for filling in last minute. I know Drew really appreciates it."

"No problem at all. It's easy work." He scowls and pulls at the collar of his shirt. "I just wish I didn't have to wear this damn thing. Hate having shit on my neck."

I can't help but chuckle, because I obviously know exactly how he's feeling, but I give him some shit anyway. "Toughen up and quit your bitching."

Gage points to my loosened collar and retorts. "Shut the fuck up! Where the hell is your tie?"

I grin broadly. "I don't work for my brother so I'll wear whatever the hell I want."

We both laugh and take a couple more drinks in silence before Gage points his bottle toward the stage. "Looks like Drew might be getting ready to speak, so I'm going to go find a good spot."

"Okay, look me up after if you want to get another drink." I tip my bottle at him in goodbye and turn to see if I can find Hannah, Drew's wife. Scanning the crowd in front of the stage, I spot her and work my way over, a smile breaking across her face as she sees me, her hand lifting to wave me over.

I wave back and only miss half a beat in my step when I notice the woman in gold is standing next to Hannah, her features a mask of surprise as I approach and kiss Hannah on the cheek. "How's my favorite sister-in-law?"

She kisses me back and giggles. "I'm your only sister-in-law."

"Then you win, hands down." I give her a wink and move to address the three people standing next to her, my eyes landing on my mystery woman, who is shaking her head, a small grin of defeat on her mouth. "Hi, I'm Ben, Hannah's brother-in-law. I don't think we've met before."

"Oh, I'm sorry Ben." Hannah shifts quickly into hostess mode. "This is Drew's friend from college, Mika Kingsley, and his new bride, Raeva." She gives me a quick look of apology. "I thought you may have already known him."

"No worries at all, Hannah." I grasp Mika's firm grip in my own and shake it. "Nice to meet you both." I give a warm smile to his wife and then move my attention to the woman in gold on her right, extending my hand, unable to hide the devil in my grin. "And you are?"

She purses her lips and tilts her head, gracefully placing her hand in mine before finally bringing her eyes up to meet mine. "Jill Baldwin. Nice to meet you, Ben."

Want more?

You can download Breaking Benjamin here: **books2read.**

com/u/bW9Z0I

Made in the USA
Columbia, SC
17 September 2021